Anthony Hope

Comedies of Courtship

Anthony Hope

Comedies of Courtship

ISBN/EAN: 9783744779098

Printed in Europe, USA, Canada, Australia, Japan

Cover: Foto ©Andreas Hilbeck / pixelio.de

More available books at **www.hansebooks.com**

Comedies of Courtship.

BY

ANTHONY HOPE.

"It is a familiar fact that the intensity of a passion varies with the proximity of the appropriate object."— Mr. Leslie Stephen's *Science of Ethics.*

"How the devil is it that fresh features
Have such a charm for us poor human creatures?"
—Lord Byron's *Don Juan.*

LONDON:

A. D. INNES & CO.,

BEDFORD STREET.

1896.

CONTENTS.

COMEDIES OF COURTSHIP.

THE WHEEL OF LOVE.

CHAPTER I.

THE VIRTUOUS HYPOCRITES.

AT first sight they had as little reason for being unhappy as it is possible to have in a world half full of sorrow. They were young and healthy; half a dozen times each had declared the other more than commonly good-looking; they both had, and never knew what it was not to have, money enough for comfort and, in addition, that divine little superfluity wherefrom joys are born. The house was good to look at and good to live in; there were horses to ride, the river to go a-rowing on, and a big box from Mudie's every week. No one worried them; Miss

B

Bussey was generally visiting the poor, or, as was the case at this moment, asleep in her armchair, with Paul, the terrier, in his basket beside her, and the cat on her lap. Lastly, they were plighted lovers, and John was staying with Miss Bussey for the express purpose of delighting and being delighted by his *fiancée*, Mary Travers. For these and all their mercies certainly they should have been truly thankful.

However, the heart of man is wicked. This fact alone can explain why Mary sat sadly in the drawing-room, feeling a letter that was tucked inside her waistband, and John strode moodily up and down the gravel walk, a cigar, badly bitten, between his teeth, and his hand ever and again covertly stealing toward his breast-pocket and pressing a scented note that lay there. In the course of every turn John would pass the window of the drawing-room; then Mary would look up with a smile and blow him a kiss, and he nodded and laughed, and returned the salute. But, the window passed, both sighed deeply and returned to fingering those hidden missives.

"Poor little girl! I must keep it up," said John.

"Dear good John! He must never know," thought Mary.

And the two fell to thinking just what was remarked a few lines back, namely, that the human heart is very wicked; they were shocked at themselves; the young often are.

Miss Bussey awoke, sat up, evicted the cat, and found her spectacles.

"Where are those children?" said she. "Billing and cooing somewhere, I suppose. Bless me, why don't they get tired of it?"

They had; not indeed of billing and cooing in general, for no one at their age does or ought to get tired of that; but of billing and cooing with one another.

It will be observed that the situation promised well for a tragedy. Nevertheless this is not the story of an unhappy marriage.

If there be one thing which Government should forbid, it is a secret engagement. Engagements should be advertised as marriages are; but unless we happen to be persons of social importance or considerable notoriety, no such precautions are taken. Of course there are engagement rings; but a man never knows one when he sees it on a lady's hand—it would indeed be impertinent to look too closely—and when he goes out alone he generally puts his in his pocket, considering that the evening will thus be rendered more enjoyable. The Ashforth-Travers engagement was not a secret now, but it had been, and had been too long. Hence, when Mary went to Scotland and met Charlie Ellerton, and when John went to Switzerland and met Dora Bellairs—the truth is, they ought never to have separated, and Miss Bussey, who was one of the people in the secret, had been quite right when she remarked that it seemed a curious arrangement. John and Mary had scoffed at the idea of a few weeks' absence having any effect on their feelings except, if indeed it were possible, that of intensifying them.

"I really think I ought to go and find them," said Miss Bussey. "Come, Paul!"

She took a parasol, for the April sun was bright, and went into the garden. When she came to the drawing-room window John was away at the end of the walk. She looked at him : he was reading a letter. She looked in at the window : Mary was reading a letter.

"Well!" exclaimed Miss Bussey. "Have they had a tiff?" And she slowly waddled (truth imposes this word—she was very stout) toward the unconscious John. He advanced toward her, still reading; not only did he not see her, but he failed to notice that Paul had got under his feet. He fell over Paul, and as he stumbled the letter fluttered out of his hand. Paul seized it, and began to toss it about in great glee.

"Good doggie!" cried Miss Bussey. "Come then! Bring it to me, dear. Good Paul!"

John's face was distorted with agony. He darted toward Paul, fell on him, and gripped him closely. Paul yelped, and Miss Bussey observed, in an indignant tone, that John need not throttle the dog. John muttered something.

"Is the letter so very precious?" asked his hostess ironically.

"Precious!" cried John. "Yes!—No!—It's nothing at all."

But he opened Paul's mouth and took out his treasure with wonderful care.

"And why," inquired Miss Bussey, "are you not with Mary, young man? You're very neglectful."

"Neglectful! Surely, Miss Bussey, you haven't noticed anything like neglect? Don't say—— "

"Bless the boy! I was only joking. You're a model lover."

"Thank you, thank you. I'll go to her at once," and he sped towards the window, opened it and walked up to Mary. Miss Bussey followed him and arrived just in time to see the lovers locked in one another's arms, their faces expressing all appropriate rapture.

"There's nothing much wrong," said Miss Bussey; wherein Miss Bussey herself was much wrong.

"What a shame! I've left you alone for more than an hour!" said John. "Have you been very unhappy?" and he added, "darling." It sounded like an afterthought.

"I have been rather unhappy," answered Mary, and her answer was true. As she said it she tucked in a projecting edge of her letter. John had hurriedly slipped his—it was rather the worse for its mauling—into his trousers-pocket.

"You—you didn't think me neglectful?"

"Oh, no."

"I was thinking of you all the time."

"And I was thinking of you, dear."

"Are you very happy?"

"Yes, John; aren't you?"

"Of course I am. Happy! I should think so;" and he kissed her with unimpeachable fervour.

When a conscientious person makes up his mind that he ought, for good reasons, to deceive somebody, there is no one like him for thorough-paced hypocrisy. When two conscientious people resolve to deceive one another, on grounds of duty, the acme of duplicity is in a fair way to be reached. John Ashforth and Mary Travers illustrated this proposition. The former had been all his life a good son, and was now a trustworthy partner, to his father, who justly relied no less on his character than on his brains. The latter, since her parents' early death had left her to her aunt's care, had been the comfort and prop of Miss Bussey's life. It is difficult to describe good people without making them seem dull; but luckily Nature is defter than novelists, and it is quite possible to be good without being dull. Neither Mary nor John was dull; a trifle limited, perhaps, they were, a thought severe in their judgments of others as well as of themselves, a little exacting with their friends and more than a little with themselves. One description paints them both; doubtless their harmony of mind had contributed more than Mary's sweet expression and finely cut features, or John's upstanding six feet and honest capable face, to produce that attachment between them which had, six months before this story begins, culminated in their engagement. Once arrived at, this ending seemed to have been inevitable. Everybody discovered that they had foretold it from the first, and modestly disclaimed any credit for anticipating a union between a couple so obviously made for one another.

The distress into which lovers such as these fell when they discovered by personal experience that sincerely to vow eternal love is one thing, and sincerely to give it quite another, may well be imagined, and may well be left to be imagined. They both went through a terrible period of temptation, wherein they listened longingly to the seductive pleading of their hearts; but both emerged triumphant, resolved to stifle their mad fancy, to prefer good faith to mere inclination, and to avoid, at all costs, wounding one to whom they had sworn to be true. Thus far their steadfastness carried them, but not beyond. They could part from their loved ones, and they did; but they could not leave them without a word. Each wrote, after leaving Scotland and Switzerland respectively, a few lines of adieu, confessing the love they felt, but with resolute sadness saying farewell for ever. They belonged to another.

It was the answers that Mary and John were reading when Miss Bussey discovered them.

Mary's ran —

"MY DEAR MISS TRAVERS,

"I have received your letter. I can't tell you what it means to me. You say all must be over between us. Don't be offended—but I won't say that yet. It can't be your duty to marry a man you don't love. You forbid me to write or come to you; and you ask only for a word of good-bye. I won't say good-bye. I'll say *Au revoir—au revoir*, my darling.

"CHARLIE.

"Burn this."

This was John's—

"MY DEAR MR. ASHFORTH,

"What am I to say to you? Oh, why, why didn't you tell me before? I oughtn't to say that, but it is too late to conceal anything from *you*. Yes, you are right. It must be good-bye. Yes, I will try to forget you. But oh, John, it's very, very, *very* difficult. I don't know how to sign this —so I won't. You'll know who it comes from, won't you? Good-bye. Burn this."

These letters, no doubt, make it plain that there had been at least a momentary weakness both in Mary and in John; but in a true and charitable view their conduct in rising superior to temptation finally was all the more remarkable and praiseworthy. They had indeed, for the time, been carried away. Even now Mary found it hard not to make allowances for herself, little as she was prone to weakness, when she thought of the impetuous *abandon* and conquering whirl with which Charlie Ellerton had wooed her; and John confessed that flight alone, a hasty flight from Interlaken after a certain evening spent in gazing at the Jungfrau, had saved him from casting everything to the winds and yielding to the slavery of Dora Bellairs's sunny smiles and charming coquetries. He had always thought that that sort of girl had no attractions for him, just as Mary had despised " butterfly-men " like Charlie Ellerton. Well, they were wrong.

The only comfort was that shallow natures felt these sorrows less; it would have broken Mary's heart (thought John), or John's (thought Mary), but Dora and Charlie would soon find consolation in another. But here, oddly enough, John generally swore heartily, and Mary always began to search for her handkerchief.

"They're as affectionate as one could wish when they're together," mused Miss Bussey, as she stroked the cat, "but at other times they're gloomy company. I suppose they can't be happy apart. Dear! dear!" And the good lady fell to wondering whether she had ever been so foolish herself.

CHAPTER II.

SYMPATHY IN SORROW.

"Give me," observed Sir Roger Deane, "Cannes, a fine day, a good set to look at, a beehive chair, a good cigar, a cocktail on one side and a nice girl on the other, and there I am! I don't want anything else."

General Bellairs pulled his white moustache and examined Sir Roger's figure and surroundings with a smile.

"Then only Lady Deane is wanting to your complete happiness," said he.

"Maud is certainly a nice girl, but when she deserts me——"

"Where is she?"

"I don't know."

"I do," interposed a young man, who wore an eye-glass and was in charge of a large jug. "She's gone to Monte."

"I might have known," said Sir Roger. "Being missed here always means you've gone to Monte—like not being at church means you've gone to Brighton."

"Surely she doesn't play?" asked the General.

"Not she! She's going to put it in a book. She writes books, you know. She put me in the last—made me a dashed fool, too, by Jove!"

"That was unkind," said the General, "from your wife."

"Oh, Lord love you, she didn't mean it. I was the hero. That's how I came to be such an ass. The dear girl meant everything that was kind. Who's taken her to Monte?"

"Charlie Ellerton," said the young man with the eye-glass.

"There! I told you she was a kind girl. She's trying to pull old Charlie up a peg or two. He's had the deuce of a facer, you know."

"I thought he seemed less cheerful than usual."

"Oh, rather. He met a girl somewhere or other—I always forget places—Miss—Miss—hang it, I can't remember names—and got awfully smitten, and everything went pleasantly and she took to him like anything, and at last

old Charlie spoke up like a man, and——"
Sir Roger paused dramatically.

" Well? " asked the General.

" She was engaged to another fellow.
Rough, wasn't it? She told old Charlie she
liked him infernally, but promises were promises, don't you know, and she'd thank him
to take his hook. And he had to take it, by
gad! Rough, don't you know? So Maud's
been cheering him up. The devil! "

" What's the matter now? " inquired the
General.

" Why, I've just remembered that I promised to say nothing about it. I say, don't
you repeat it, General, nor you either,
Laing."

The General laughed.

" Well," said Sir Roger, " he oughtn't to
have been such a fool as to tell me. He
knows I never remember to keep things dark.
It's not my fault."

A girl came out of the hotel and strolled
up to where the group was. She was dark,
slight, and rather below middle height ; her
complexion at this moment was a trifle sallow
and her eyes listless, but it seemed rather as
though she had dressed her face into a tragic
cast, the set of the features being naturally

mirthful. She acknowledged the men's salutations and sat down with a sigh.

"Not on to-day?" asked Sir Roger, waving his cigar toward the lawn-tennis courts.

"No," said Miss Bellairs.

"Are you seedy, Dolly?" inquired the General.

"No," said Miss Bellairs.

Mr. Laing fixed his eye-glass and surveyed the young lady.

"Are you taking any?" said he, indicating the jug.

"I don't see any fun in vulgarity," observed Miss Bellairs.

The General smiled. Sir Roger's lips assumed the shape for a whistle.

"That's a nasty one for me," said Laing.

"Ah, here you are, Roger," exclaimed a fresh clear voice from behind the chairs. "I've been looking for you everywhere. We've seen everything—Mr. Ellerton was most kind—and I do so want to tell you my impressions."

The new-comer was Lady Deane, a tall young woman, plainly dressed in a serviceable cloth walking-gown. By her side stood Charlie Ellerton in a flannel suit of pronounced striping; he wore a little yellow moustache, had blue eyes and curly hair, and his face was tanned a wholesome ruddy-brown. He looked very melancholy.

"Letters from Hell," murmured Sir Roger.

"But I was so distressed," continued his wife. "Mr. Ellerton would gamble, and he lost ever so much money."

"A fellow must amuse himself," remarked Charlie gloomily, and with apparent unconsciousness he took a glass from Laing and drained it.

"Gambling and drink—what does that mean?" asked Sir Roger.

"Shut up, Deane," said Charlie.

Miss Bellairs rose suddenly and walked away. Her movement expressed impatience with her surroundings. After a moment Charlie Ellerton slowly sauntered after her. She sat down on a garden-seat some way off. Charlie placed himself at the opposite end. A long pause ensued.

"I'm afraid I'm precious poor company," said Charlie.

"I didn't want you to be company at all," answered Miss Bellairs, and she sloped her parasol until it obstructed his view of her face.

"I'm awfully sorry, but I can't stand the sort of rot Deane and Laing are talking."

"Can't you? Neither can I."

"They never seem to be serious about anything, you know." Charlie sighed deeply, and for three minutes there was silence.

"Do you know Scotland at all?" asked Charlie at last.

"Only a little."

"There last year?"

"No, I was in Switzerland."

"Oh."

"Do you know Interlaken?"

"No."

"Oh."

"May I have a cigarette?"

"Of course, if you like."

Charlie lit his cigarette and smoked silently for a minute or two.

"I call this a beastly place," said he.

"Yes, horrid," she answered, and the force of sympathy made her move the parasol and turn her face towards her companion. "But I thought," she continued, "you came here every spring?"

"Oh, I don't mind the place so much. It's the people."

"Yes, isn't it? I know what you mean."

"You can't make a joke of everything, can you?"

"Indeed no," sighed Dora.

Charlie looked at his cigarette, and, his eyes carefully fixed on it, said in a timid tone,

"What's the point, for instance, of talking as if love was all bosh?"

Dora's parasol swept down again swiftly, but Charlie was still looking at the cigarette and he did not notice its descent, nor could he see that Miss Bellairs's cheek was no longer sallow.

"It's such cheap rot," he continued, "and when a fellow's—I say, Miss Bellairs, I'm not boring you?"

The parasol wavered and finally moved.

"No," said Miss Bellairs.

"I don't know whether you—no, I mustn't say that; but I know what it is to be in love, Miss Bellairs; but what's the good of talking about it? Everybody laughs."

Miss Bellairs put down her parasol.

"I shouldn't laugh," she said softly. "It's horrid to laugh at people when they're in trouble," and her eyes were very sympathetic.

"You are kind. I don't mind talking about it to you. You know I'm not the sort of fellow who falls in love with every girl he meets; so of course it's worse when I do."

" Was it just lately ? " murmured Dora.

" Last summer."

" Ah ! And—and didn't she——? "

" Oh, I don't know. Yes, hang it, I believe she did. She was perfectly straight, Miss Bellairs. I don't say a word against her. She—I think she didn't know her own feelings until—until I spoke, you know—and then—— "

" Do go on, if—if it doesn't—— "

" Why, then, the poor girl cried and said it couldn't be because she—she was engaged to another fellow ; and she sent me away."

Miss Bellairs was listening attentively.

" And," continued Charlie, " she wrote and said it must be good-bye and—and—— "

" And you think she——? "

" She told me so," whispered Charlie. " She said she couldn't part without telling me. Oh, I say, Miss Bellairs, isn't it all damnable ? I beg your pardon."

Dora was tracing little figures on the gravel with her parasol.

" Now what would you do ? " cried Charlie. " She loves me, I know she does, and she's going to marry this other fellow because she promised him first. I don't suppose she knew what love was then."

" Oh, I'm sure she didn't," exclaimed Dora earnestly.

" You can't blame her, you know. And it's absurd to—to—to—not to—well, to marry a fellow you don't care for when you care for another fellow, you know ! "

" Yes."

" Of course you can hardly imagine yourself in that position, but suppose a man liked you and—and was placed like that, you know, what should you feel you ought to do ? "

" Oh, I don't know," exclaimed Dora, clasping her hands. " Oh, do tell me what you think ! I'd give the world to know ! "

Charlie's surprised glance warned her of her betrayal.

" You mustn't ask me," she exclaimed hastily.

" I won't ask a word. I—I'm awfully sorry, Miss Bellairs."

" Nobody knows," she murmured.

" Nobody shall through me."

" You're not very—? I'm very ashamed."

" Why? And because of me ! After what I've told you ! "

Charlie rose suddenly.

" I'm not going to stand it," he announced.

Dora looked up eagerly.

"What? You're going to—— ?"

"I'm going to have a shot at it. Am I to stand by and see her——? I'm hanged if I do. Could that be right?"

"I should like to know what one's *duty* is."

"This talk with you has made me quite clear. We've reasoned it out, you see. They're not to be married for two or three months. A lot can be done in that time."

"Ah, you're a man!"

"I shall write first. If that doesn't do, I shall go to her."

Dora shook her head mournfully.

"Now, look here, Miss Bellairs—you don't mind me advising you?"

"I ought not to have let you see, but as it is—— "

"You do as I do, you stick to it. Confound it, you know, when one's life's happiness is at stake—— "

"Oh, yes, yes!"

"One mustn't be squeamish, must one?"

And Dora Bellairs, in a very low whisper, answered, "No."

"I shall write to-night."

"Oh! To-night?"

"Yes.   Now promise me you will too."

"It's harder for me than you."

"Not if he really——"

"Oh, indeed, he really does, Mr. Ellerton."

"Then you'll write ? "

"Perhaps."

"No.   Promise ! "

"Well—it must be right.   Yes, I will."

"I feel the better for our talk, Miss Bellairs—don't you ? "

"I do a little."

"We shall be friends now, you know; even if I bring it off I shan't be content unless you do too.   Won't you give me your good wishes ? "

"Indeed I will."

"Shake hands on it."

They shook hands and began to stroll back to the tennis-courts.

"They look a little better," observed Sir Roger Deane, who had been listening to an eloquent description of the gaming-tables.

Dora and Charlie walked on towards the hotel.

"Hi ! " shouted Sir Roger.   "Tea's coming out here."

"I've got a letter to write," said Charlie.

" Well, Miss Bellairs, you must come. Who's to pour it out ? "

"I must catch the post, Sir Roger," answered Dora.

They went into the house together. In the hall they parted.

" You'll let me know what happens, Mr. Ellerton, won't you ?   I'm so interested."

" And you ? "

" Oh—well, perhaps ; " and the sallow of her cheeks had turned to a fine dusky red as she ran upstairs.

Thus it happened that a second letter for John Ashforth and a second letter for Mary Travers left Cannes that night.

And if it seems a curious coincidence that Dora and Charlie should meet at Cannes, it can only be answered that they were each of them just as likely to be at Cannes as anywhere else.   Besides, who knows that these things are all coincidence ?

CHAPTER III.

A PROVIDENTIAL DISCLOSURE.

On Wednesday, the eleventh of April, John Ashforth rose from his bed full of a great and momentous resolution. There is nothing very strange in that, perhaps; it is just the time of day when such things come to a man, and, in ordinary cases, they are very prone to disappear with the relics of breakfast. But John was of sterner stuff. He had passed a restless night, tossed to and fro by very disturbing gusts of emotion, and he arose with the firm conviction that if he would escape shipwreck he must secure his bark by immovable anchors while he was, though not in honour, yet in law and fact, free; he could not trust himself. Sorrowfully admitting his weakness, he turned to the true, the right, the heroic remedy.

"I'll marry Mary to-day fortnight," said he. "When we are man and wife I shall forget this madness, and love her as I used to."

He went down to breakfast, ate a bit of toast and drank a cup of very strong tea. Presently Mary appeared and greeted him with remarkable tenderness. His heart smote him, and his remorse strengthened his determination.

"I want to speak to you after breakfast," he told her.

His manner was so significant that a sudden gleam of hope flashed into her mind. Could it be that he had seen, that he would be generous? She banished the shameful hope. She would not accept generosity at the expense of pain to him.

Miss Bussey, professing to find bed the best place in the world, was in the habit of taking her breakfast there. The lovers were alone, and, the meal ended, they passed together into the conservatory. Mary sat down, and John leant against the glass door, opposite to her.

"Well?" said she, smiling at him.

It suddenly struck John that, in a scene of this nature, it ill-befitted him to stand three yards from the lady. He took a chair and drew it close beside her. The thing had to be done and it should be done properly.

"We've made a mistake, Mary," he

announced, taking her hand and speaking in a rallying tone.

"A mistake!" she cried; "oh, how?"

"In fixing our marriage——"

"So soon?"

"My darling!" said John (and it was impossible to deny admiration to the tone he said it in). "No. So late! What are we waiting for? Why are we wasting all this precious time?"

Mary could not speak, but consternation passed for an appropriate confusion, and John pursued his passionate pleadings. As Mary felt his grasp and looked into his honest eyes, her duty lay plain before her. She would not stoop to paltry excuses on the score of clothes, invitations, or such trifles. She had made up her mind to the thing; surely she ought to do it in the way most gracious and most pleasing to her lover.

"If aunt consents," she murmured at last, "do as you like, John dear," and the embrace which each felt to be inevitable at such a crisis passed between them.

A discreet cough separated them. The butler stood in the doorway, with two letters on a salver. One he handed to Mary, the other to John, and walked away with a twinkle in his eye. However, even our butlers do not know everything that happens in our houses (to say nothing of our hearts), although they may think they do.

John looked at his letter, started violently and crushed it into his pocket. He glanced at Mary; her letter lay neglected on her lap. She was looking steadily out of the window.

"Well, that's settled," said John. "I—I think I'll have a cigar, dear."

"Yes, do, darling," said Mary; and John went out.

These second letters were unfortunately so long as to make it impossible to reproduce them. They were also very affecting, Dora's from its pathos, Charlie's from its passion. But the waves of emotion beat fruitlessly on the rock-built walls of conscience. At almost the same moment, Mary, brushing away a tear, and John, blowing his nose, sat down to write a brief, a final answer. "We are to be married to-day fortnight," they said. They closed the envelopes without a moment's delay and went to drop their letters in the box. The servant was already waiting to go to the post with them, and a second later the fateful documents were on their way to Cannes.

" Now," said John, with a ghastly smile, " we can have a glorious long day together ! "

Mary was determined to leave herself no loophole.

" We must tell aunt what—what we have decided upon this morning," she reminded him. " It means that the wedding must be very quiet."

" I shan't mind that. Shall you ? "

"I shall like it of all things," she answered. " Come and find Aunt Sarah."

Miss Bussey had always—or at least for a great many years back—maintained the general proposition that young people do not know their own minds. This morning's news confirmed her opinion.

" Why; the other day you both agreed that the middle of June would do perfectly. Now you want it all done in a scramble."

The pair stood before her, looking very guilty.

" What is the meaning of this—this "—she very nearly said "indecent "—" extraordinary haste ? "

Miss Bussey asked only one indulgence from her friends. Before she did a kind thing she liked to be allowed to say one or two sharp ones. Her niece was aware of this fancy of hers and took refuge in silence. John, less experienced in his hostess's ways, launched into the protests appropriate to an impatient lover.

"Well," said Miss Bussey, "I must say you look properly ashamed of yourself" (John certainly did), "so I'll see what can be done. What a fluster we shall live in! Upon my word you might as well have it to-morrow. The fuss would have been no worse and a good deal shorter."

The next few days passed, as Miss Bussey had predicted, in a fluster. Mary was running after dressmakers, John after licences, Cook's tickets, a best man, and all the *impedimenta* of a marriage. The intercourse of the lovers was much interrupted, and to this Miss Bussey attributed the low spirits that Mary sometimes displayed.

"There, there, my dear," she would say impatiently—for the cheerful old lady hated long faces—"you'll have enough of him and to spare by-and-by."

Curiously this point of view did not comfort Mary. She liked John very much, she esteemed him even more than she liked him, he would, she thought, have made an ideal brother. Ah, why had she not made a brother

of him while there was time? Then she
would have enjoyed his constant friendship
all her life; for it was not with him, as with
that foolish boy Charlie, all or nothing. John
was reasonable; he would not have threat-
ened—well, reading his letter one way, Charlie
almost seemed to be tampering with propriety.
John would never have done that. And these
reflections, all of which should have pleaded
for John, ended in tears over the lost charms
of Charlie.

One evening, just a week before the wedding, she roused herself from some such sad
meditations, and, duty-driven, sought John in
the smoking-room. The door was half open
and she entered noiselessly. John was sitting
at the table; his arms were outspread on it,
and his face buried in his hands. Thinking
he was asleep, she approached on tiptoe and
leant over his shoulder. As she did so her
eyes fell on a sheet of notepaper; it was
clutched in John's right hand, and the en-
circling grasp covered it, save at the top.
The top was visible, and Mary, before she
knew what she was doing, had read the em-
bossed heading—nothing else, just the em-
bossed heading—*Hôtel de Luxe, Cannes, Alpes
Maritimes.*

The drama teaches us how often a guilty mind rushes, on some trifling cause, to self-revelation. Like a flash came the conviction that Charlie had written to John, that her secret was known, and John's heart broken. In a moment she fell on her knees crying,

" Oh, how wicked I've been! Forgive me, do forgive me ! Oh, John, can you forgive me ? "

John was not asleep, he also was merely meditating ; but if he had been a very Rip Van Winkle this cry of agony would have roused him. He started violently—as well he might—from his seat, looked at Mary, and crumpled the letter into a shapeless ball.

" You didn't see ? " he asked hoarsely.

" No, but I know. I mean I saw the heading, and knew it must be from him. Oh, John ! "

" From *him !* "

" Yes. He's—he's staying there. Oh, John ! Really I'll never see or speak to him again. Really I won't. Oh, you can trust me, John. See ! I'll hide nothing. Here's his letter ! You see I've sent him away ? "

And she took from her pocket Charlie's letter, and in her noble fidelity (to John—the less we say about poor Charlie the better) handed it to him.

"What's this?" asked John, in bewilderment. "Who's it from?"

"Charlie Ellerton," she stammered.

"Who's Charlie Ellerton? I never heard—but am I to read it?"

"Yes, please, I—I think you'd better."

John read it; Mary followed his eyes, and the moment they reached the end, without giving him time to speak, she exclaimed,

"There, you see I spoke the truth. I had sent him away. What does he say to you, John?"

"I never heard of him in my life before."

"John! Then who is your letter from?"

He hesitated. He felt an impulse to imitate her candour, but prudence suggested that he should be sure of his ground first.

"Tell me all," he said, sitting down. "Who is this man, and what has he to do with you?"

"Why don't you show me his letter? I don't know what he's said about me."

"What could he say about you?"

"Well, he—he might say that—that I cared for him, John."

"And do you?" demanded John, and his voice was anxious.

Duty demanded a falsehood; Mary did her

best to satisfy its imperious commands. It was no use.

"Oh, John," she murmured, and then began to cry.

For a moment wounded pride struggled with John's relief; but then a glorious vision of what this admission of Mary's might mean to him swept away his pique.

"Read this," he said, giving her Dora Bellairs' letter, "and then we'll have an explanation."

Half an hour later Miss Bussey was roused from a pleasant snooze. John and Mary stood beside her, hand in hand. They were brother and sister now—that was an integral part of the arrangement—and so they stood hand in hand. Their faces were radiant.

"We came to tell you, auntie dear, that we have decided that we're not suited to one another," began Mary.

"Not at all," said John decisively.

Miss Bussey stared helplessly from one to the other.

"It's all right, Miss Bussey," remarked John cheerfully. "We've had an explanation; we part by mutual consent."

"John," said Mary, "is to be just my

brother and I his sister. Oh, and, auntie, I want to go with him to Cannes."

This last suggestion, which naturally did not appear to any well-regulated mind to harmonise with what had gone before, restored voice to Miss Bussey.

" What's the matter with you? Are you mad ? " she demanded.

John sat down beside her. His friends anticipated a distinguished Parliamentary career for John; he could make anything sound reasonable. Miss Bussey was fascinated by his suave and fluent narrative of what had befallen Mary and himself; she could not but admire his just remarks on the providential disclosure of the true state of the case before it was too late, and sympathised with the picture of suffering nobly suppressed which grew under his skilful hand; she was inflamed when he ardently declared his purpose of seeking out Dora; she was touched when he kissed Mary's hand and declared that the world held no nobler woman. Before John's eloquence even the stern facts of a public engagement, of invited guests, of dresses ordered and presents received, lost their force, and the romantic spirit, rekindled, held un-divided sway in Miss Bussey's heart.

"But," she said, "why does Mary talk of going to Cannes with you ?"

"Mr. Ellerton is at Cannes, aunt," murmured Mary shyly.

"But you can't travel with John."

"Oh, but you must come too."

"It looks as if you were running after him."

"I'll chance Charlie thinking that," cried Mary, clasping her hands in glee.

Miss Bussey pretended to be reluctant to undertake the journey, but she was really quite ready to yield, and soon everything was settled on the new basis.

"And now to write and tell people," said Miss Bussey. "That's the worst part of it."

"Poor dear ! We'll help," cried Mary. "But I must write to Cannes."

"Wire !" cried John.

"Of course, wire !" echoed Mary.

"The first thing to-morrow."

"Before breakfast."

"Mary, I shall never forget——"

"No, John, it's you who——" and they went off in a torrent of mutual laudation.

Miss Bussey shook her head.

"If they think all that of one another, why don't they marry ?" she said.

CHAPTER IV.

THE TALE OF A POSTMARK.

"Yes," said Lady Deane, "we leave to-day week; Roger has to be back the first week in May, and I want to stop at one or two places *en roûte.*"

"Let's see. To-day's the 19th, no, the 20th; there's nothing to remind one of time here. That'll be the 27th. That's about my date; we might go together if you and Deane have no objection."

"Oh, I should be delighted, General; and shall you stay at all in Paris?"

"A few days—just to show Dolly the sights."

"How charming! And you and I must have some expeditions together. Roger is so odd about not liking to take me."

"We'll do the whole thing, Lady Deane," answered General Bellairs heartily. "Notre Dame, Versailles, the Invalides, Eiffel Tower."

Lady Deane's broad white brow showed a little pucker.

"That wasn't quite what I meant," said she. "Oh, but Roger could take Dora to those, couldn't he, while you and I made a point of seeing some of the real life of the people? Of studying them in their ordinary resorts, their places of recreation and amusement."

"Oh, the Français, and the opera, and so on, of course."

"No, no, no," exclaimed Lady Deane, tapping her foot impatiently and fixing her grey eyes on the General's now puzzled face. "Not the same old treadmill in Paris as in London! Not that, General!"

"What then, my dear lady?" asked he. "Your wish is law to me," and it was true that he had become very fond of his earnest young friend. "What do you want to see? The Chamber of Deputies?"

Sir Roger's voice struck in.

"I'm not a puritanical husband, Bellairs, but I must make a stand somewhere. *Not* the Chamber of Deputies."

"Don't be silly, Roger dear," said Lady Deane, in her usual tone of dispassionate · reproof.

"I can't find out where she does want to go to," remarked the General.

"I can tell you," said Sir Roger; and he leant down and whispered a name in the General's ear. The General jumped.

"Good heavens!" he exclaimed. "I haven't been there since the fifties. Is it still like what it used to be?"

"How should I know?" inquired Sir Roger. "I'm not a student of social phenomena. Maud is, so she wants to go."

Lady Deane was looking on with a quiet smile.

"She never mentioned it," protested the General.

"Oh, of course if there's a worse place now!" conceded Sir Roger.

"I'll make up my mind when we arrive," observed Lady Deane. "Anyhow, I shall rely on you, General."

The General looked a little uncomfortable.

"If Deane doesn't object——"

"I shouldn't think of taking my wife to such places."

Suddenly Dora Bellairs rushed up to them.

"Have you seen Mr. Ellerton?" she cried. "Where is he?"

"In the smoking-room," answered Sir Roger. "Do you want him?"

"Would you mind? I can't go in there: it's full of *men*."

"After all we must be somewhere," pleaded Sir Roger, as he went on his errand.

"Dolly," said the General, "I've just made a charming arrangement. Lady Deane and Sir Roger start for Paris to-day week, and we're going with them. You said you'd like another week here."

"It's charming our being able to go together, isn't it?" said Lady Deane.

Dora's face did not express rapture, yet she liked the Deanes very much.

"Oh, but——" she began.

"Well?" asked her father.

"I rather want to go a little sooner."

"I'm afraid," said Lady Deane, "we shan't get Roger to move before then. He's bent on seeing the tennis tournament through. When did you want to go, Dora?"

"Well, in fact—to-night."

"My dear Dolly, what a weathercock you are! It's impossible. I'm dining with the Grand Duke on Monday. You must make up your mind to stay, young woman."

"Oh, please, papa——"

"But why do you want to go?" asked the General, rather impatiently.

Dora had absolutely no producible reason for her eagerness to go. And yet—oh, if they only knew what was at stake! "We're to be married in a fortnight!" She could see the words dancing before her eyes. And she must waste a precious week here!

"Do you want me, Miss Bellairs?" asked Charlie Ellerton, coming up to them.

"Yes. I want—oh, I want to go to Rumpelmayer's."

"All right. Come along. I'm delighted to go with you."

They walked off in silence. Dora was in distress. She saw that the General was immovable.

Suddenly Charlie turned to her and remarked, "Well, it's all over with me, Miss Bellairs."

"What? How do you mean?"

"My chance is gone. They're to be married in a fortnight. I had a letter to say so this morning."

Dora turned suddenly to him.

"Oh, but it's too extraordinary," she cried. "So had I!"

"What?"

" Why, a letter to say they were to be married in a fortnight."

" Nonsense ! "

" Yes.   Mr. Ellerton—who—who is your friend ? "

" Her name's Mary Travers."

" And who is she going to marry ? "

" Ah, she hasn't told me that."

A suspicion of the truth struck them both. Charlie produced his letter.

" She writes," he said, showing the post-mark, " from Dittington."

" It is ! It is ! " she cried. " It must be Mary Travers that Mr. Ashforth is going to marry ! "

" Is that your friend ? "

" Yes.   Is she pretty, Mr. Ellerton ? "

" Oh, awfully.   What sort of a fellow is he ? "

" Splendid ! "

" Isn't it a deuced queer thing ? "

" Most extraordinary.   And when we told one another we never thought—— "

" How could we ? "

" Well, no, we couldn't, of course."

A pause followed.   Then Charlie observed, " I suppose there's nothing to be done."

" Nothing to be done, Mr. Ellerton !   Why,

if I were a man, I'd leave for England to-night."

"And why can't you?"

"Papa won't. But you might."

"Ye-es, I suppose I might. It would look rather odd, wouldn't it?"

"Why, you yourself suggested it!"

"Yes, but the marriage was a long way off then."

"There's the more reason now for haste."

"Of course, that's true; but—— "

"Oh, if papa would only take me!"

A sudden idea seemed to strike Charlie; he assumed an air of chivalrous sympathy.

"When shall you go?" he asked.

"Not till to-day week," she said. "We shan't get to England till three or four days before—it." Dora knew nothing of the proposed stay in Paris.

"Look here, Miss Bellairs," said Charlie, "we agreed to stand by one another. I shall wait and go when you do."

"But think—— "

"I've thought."

"You're risking everything."

"If she'll break it off ten days before, she'll do the same four days before."

"If she really loves you she will."

" Anyhow we'll stand or fall together."

" Oh, I oughtn't to let you; but I can't refuse. How kind you are ! "

" Then that's settled," said Charlie. " And we must try to console one another till then."

" The suspense is awful, isn't it ? "

" Of course. But we must appear cheerful. We mustn't betray ourselves."

" Not for the world ! I can never thank you enough. You'll come with us all the way ? "

" Yes."

" Thank you again."

She gave him her hand, which he pressed gently.

" Hallo ! " said he. " We seem to have got up by the church somewhere. Where were we going to ? "

" Why, to Rumpelmayer's."

" Oh, ah ! Well, let's go back to the hotel."

Wonderings on the extraordinary coincidence, with an occasional reference to the tender tie of a common sorrow which bound them together, beguiled the journey back, and when they reached the hotel Dora was quite calm. Charlie seemed distinctly cheerful, and when his companion left him he sat down by Deane and remarked in a careless way, just as if he neither knew nor cared what the rest of them were going to do,

"Well, I shall light out of here in a few days. I suppose you're staying some time longer?"

"Off in a week," said Sir Roger.

"Oh, by Jove, that's about my mark. Going back to England?"

"Yes, I suppose so—ultimately. We shall stay a few days in Paris *en route*. The Bellairs go with us."

"Oh, do they?"

Sir Roger smiled gently.

"Surprised?" he asked.

Charlie ignored the question.

"And you aren't going to hurry?" he inquired.

"Why should we?"

Charlie sat silent. It was tolerably plain that, unless the few days *en route* were very few indeed, John Ashforth and Mary Travers were in a fair way to be prosperously and peacefully married before Dora Bellairs set foot in England. And if he stayed with the Bellairs, before he did, either! Charlie lit a cigarette, and sat puffing and thinking.

"Dashed nice girl, Dora Bellairs," observed Sir Roger.

"Think so?"

"I do. She's the only girl I ever saw that Laing was smitten with."

"Laing!" said Charlie.

"Well, what's the matter? He's an uncommon good chap, Laing—one of the best chaps I know—and he's got lots of coin. I don't expect she'd sneeze at Laing."

It is, no doubt, taking a very serious responsibility to upset an arrangement arrived at deliberately and carried almost to a conclusion. A man should be very sure that he can make a woman happy—happier than any other man could—before he asks her to face the turmoil and the scandal of breaking off her marriage only a week before its celebration. Sure as he may be of his own affection, he must be equally sure of hers, equally sure that their mutual love is deep and permanent. He must consider his claims to demand such a sacrifice. What remorse will be his if, afterwards, he discovers that what he did was not, in truth, for her real happiness! He must be on his guard against mere selfishness or mere vanity masquerading in the garb of a genuine passion.

As these thoughts occurred to Charlie Ellerton he felt that he was at a crisis of his life. He also felt glad that he had still a quiet week at Cannes in which to revolve these considerations in his mind. Above all, he must do nothing hastily.

Dora came out, a book in her hand. Her soft white frock fluttered in the breeze, and she pushed back a loose curl of dark hair that caressed her cheek.

"A dashed nice girl, upon my honour," said Sir Roger Deane.

"Oh, very."

"I say, old chap, I suppose you're in no hurry? You'll put in a few days in Paris? We might have a day out, mightn't we?"

"I don't know yet," said Charlie; and, when Deane left him, he sat on in solitude. Was it possible that in the space of a week——? No, it was impossible. And yet, with a girl like that——

"I did the right thing in waiting to go with her, anyhow," said Charlie, comforting himself.

CHAPTER V.

A SECOND EDITION.

" Don't you think it's an interesting sort of title ? " inquired Lady Deane of Mr. Laing.

Laing was always a little uneasy in her presence. He felt not only that she was analysing him, but that the results of the analysis seemed to her to be a very small *residuum* of solid matter. Besides, he had been told that she had described him as a " commonplace young man," a thing nobody could be expected to like.

" Capital ! " he answered, nervously fingering his eye-glass. " ' The Transformation of Giles Brockleton ! ' Capital ! "

" I think it will do," said Lady Deane complacently.

" Er—what was he transformed into, Lady Deane ? "

" A man," replied the lady emphatically.

" Of course. I see," murmured Laing

apologetically, stifling a desire to ask what Giles had been before.

A moment later the author enlightened him.

"Yes," said she, "into a man, from a useless, mischievous, contemptible idler, a parasite, Mr. Laing, a creature to whom——"

"What did it, Lady Deane?" interrupted Laing hastily. He felt somehow as if he were catalogued.

"Just a woman's influence."

Laing's face displayed relief; he felt that he was in his depth again.

"Oh, got married, you mean? Well, of course, he'd have to pull up a bit, wouldn't he? Hang it, I think it's a fellow's duty——"

"You don't quite understand me," observed Lady Deane coldly. "He did not marry the woman."

"What, did she give him the—I mean, wouldn't she have him, Lady Deane?"

"She would have married him; but beside her he saw himself in his true colours. Knowing what he was, how could he dare? That was his punishment, and punishment brought transformation."

As Lady Deane sketched her idea, her eyes kindled and her tone became animated.

Laing admired both her and her idea, and he expressed his feelings by saying,

"Remarkable sort of chap, Lady Deane. I shall read it all right, you know."

"I think you ought," said she, rising, and leaving him to wonder whether she had "meant anything."

He gave himself a little shake, as though to escape from the atmosphere of seriousness which she had diffused about him, and looked round. A little way off he saw Dora Bellairs and Charlie Ellerton sitting side by side. His brow clouded. Before Charlie came it had been his privilege to be Miss Bellairs' cavalier, and although he never hoped, nor, to tell the truth, desired more than a temporary favour in her eyes, he did not quite like being ousted.

"Pretty good for a fellow who's just got the bag!" he remarked scornfully, referring to Roger Deane's unauthorised revelation.

It was the day before the exodus to Paris. Dora's period of weary waiting had worn itself away, and she was acknowledging to Charlie that the last two or three days had passed quicker than she had ever thought they could.

"The first two days I was wretched, the

E

next two gloomy, but these last almost peaceful. In spite of—you know what—I think you've done me good on the whole."

"Don't mention it," said Charlie, flinging his arm over the back of the seat and looking at his companion.

"And now, in the end," pursued Dora, "I'm actually a little sorry to leave all this; it's so beautiful," and she waved her parasol vaguely at the hills and the islands, while with the other hand she took off her hat and allowed the breeze to blow through her hair.

"It *is* jolly, isn't it?" she asked.

"I should rather think it was," said Charlie. "The jolliest I've ever seen." It was evident that he did not refer to the scenery.

"Oh, you promised you wouldn't," cried Dora reproachfully.

"Well, then, I'll promise again," he replied, smiling amiably.

"What must I think of you, when only a week or so ago——? Oh, and what must you think of me to suppose I could? Oh, Mr. Ellerton!"

"Like to know what I think of you?" inquired Charlie, quite unperturbed by this passionate rebuke.

"Certainly not," said she, with dignity; and turned away. A moment later, however, she attacked him again.

"And you've done nothing," she said indignantly, "but suggest to papa interesting places to stop at on the way, and things he ought to see in Paris. Yes, and you actually suggested going home by sea from Marseilles. And all the time you knew it was vital to me to get home as soon as possible. To me? Yes, and to you *last week*. Shall I tell you something, Mr. Ellerton?"

"Please," said Charlie. "Whisper it in my ear;" and he offered his head in fitting proximity.

"I shouldn't mind who heard," she declared. "I despise you, Mr. Ellerton."

Charlie was roused to a protest.

"For downright unfairness give me a girl!" said he. "Here have I taken the manly course! After a short period of weakness— I admit that—I have conquered my feelings; I have determined not to distress Miss Travers by intruding on her; I have overcome the promptings of a cowardly despair; I have turned my back resolutely on a past devoid of hope. I am, after a sore struggle, myself again. And my reward, Miss Bellairs, is to be told that you despise me. Upon my honour, you'll be despising Simon Stylites next."

"And you wrote and told Miss Travers you were coming !"

"All right. I shall write and tell her I'm not coming. I shall say, Miss Bellairs, that it seems to me to be an undignified thing——"

"To do what I'm going to do? Thank you, Mr. Ellerton."

"Oh, I forgot."

"The irony of it is that you persuaded me to do it yourself."

"I was a fool; but I didn't know you so well then."

"What's that got to do with it ? "

"Everything."

"You didn't know yourself, I'm afraid," she remarked. "You thought you were a man of some—some depth of feeling, some constancy, a man whose—whose regard a girl would value, instead of being——"

"Just a poor devil who worships the ground you tread on."

Dora laughed scornfully.

"Second edition ! " said she. "The first dedicated to Miss Travers."

And then Charlie (and it is things like this which shake that faith in human nature that we try to cling to) said in a low but quite distinct voice—

"Oh, d——n Miss Travers!"

Dora shot—it almost looked as if something had shot her, as it used, in old days, Miss Zazel—up from her seat.

"I thought I was talking to a *gentleman*," said she. "I suppose you'll use that—expression—about me in a week?"

"In a good deal less, if you treat me like this," said Charlie, and his air was one of hopeless misery.

We all recollect that Anne ended by being tolerably kind to wicked King Richard. After all, Charlie had the same excuse.

"I don't want to be unkind," said Dora more gently.

"I'll do anything in the world to please you."

"Then make papa go straight to Paris, and straight on from Paris," said Dora, using her power mercilessly.

"Oh, I say, I didn't mean that, Miss Bellairs."

"You said you'd do anything I liked."

Charlie looked at her thoughtfully.

" I suppose you've no pity ? " he inquired.

" For you ? Not a bit."

" You probably don't know how beautiful you are ? "

" Don't be foolish, and—and impertinent."

She was standing opposite to him. With a sudden motion, he sprang forward, fell on one knee, seized her ungloved hand, covered it with kisses, sprang up, and hastened away, crying as he went,

" All right.   I'll do it."

Dora stood where he left her. First she looked at her hand, then at Charlie's retreating back, then again at her hand. Her cheek was flushed and she trembled a little.

" John never did that," she said, " at least, not without asking. And even then, not quite like that."

She walked on slowly, then stopped and exclaimed,

" I wonder if he ever did that to Mary Travers ! "

And her last reflection was,

" Poor boy ! He must be—oh, dear me ! "

When Charlie reached the tennis-courts, he was, considering the moving scene through which he had passed, wonderfully calm. In fact he was smiling and whistling. Espying

Sir Roger Deane, he went and sat down by him.

"Roger," said he. "I'm going with you and the Bellairs, to-morrow."

"I know that."

"Miss Bellairs wants to go straight through to England without stopping anywhere."

"She'll have to want, I expect."

"And I've promised to try and get the General to do what she wants."

"Have you though?"

"I suppose, Roger, old fellow—you know you've great influence with him—I suppose it's no use asking you to say a word to him?"

"Not a bit."

"Why?"

"Because Maud particularly wants him to stay with us in Paris."

"Oh, of course, if Lady Deane wishes it, I mustn't say a word. She's quite made up her mind about it, has she?"

"Well, I suppose so."

"She's strong on it, I mean? Not likely to change?"

"I think not, Charlie."

"She'd ask him to stay, as a favour to her?"

"I shouldn't at all wonder."

" Oh, well then, my asking him won't make much difference."

" Frankly, I don't see why it should."

" Thanks. I only wanted to know. You're not in a hurry, Roger? I mean, you won't ask your wife to go straight on ? "

" No, I shan't, Charlie. I want to stop myself."

" Thanks, old chap! See you at dinner; " and Charlie strolled off with a reassured air.

Sir Roger sat and thought.

" I see his game," he said to himself at last, " but I'm hanged if I see hers. Why does she want to get back to England? Perhaps if I delay her as much as I can, she'll tell me. Hanged if I don't! Anyhow I'm glad to see old Charlie getting convalescent."

The next morning the whole party left Cannes by the early train. The Bellairs, the Deanes, and Charlie Ellerton travelled together. Laing announced his intention of following by the afternoon train.

" Oh," said Lady Deane, " you'll get to Paris sooner than we do."

Dora looked gloomy; so did Charlie, after a momentary, hastily smothered smile.

The porter approached and asked for an

address.   They told him the Grand Hotel,
Paris.

"If anything comes to-day, I'll bring it
on," said Laing.

"Yes, do; we shall have no address before
Paris," answered General Bellairs.

They drove off, and Laing, feeling rather
solitary, returned to his cigar.   An hour
later the waiter brought him two telegrams,
one for Dora and one for Charlie.   He looked
at the addresses.

"Just too late, by Jove!   All right, garçon,
I'll take 'em ;" and he thrust them into the
pocket of his flannel jacket.   And when, after
lunch, he could not stand the dulness any
longer and went to Monte Carlo, he left the
telegrams in the discarded flannels, where
they lay till—the time when they were discovered.   For Mr. Laing clean forgot all
about them!

CHAPTER VI.

A MAN WITH A THEORY.

EVEN Miss Bussey was inclined to think that all had happened for the best. John's eloquence had shaken her first disapprobation ; the visible happiness of the persons chiefly concerned pleaded yet more persuasively. What harm, after all, was done, except for a little trouble and a little gossip ? To these Mary and John were utterly indifferent. At first they had been rather shy in referring, before one another, to their loves, but custom taught them to mention the names without confusion, and ere long they had exchanged confidences as to their future plans. John's arrangement was obviously the more prudent and becoming. He discountenanced Mary's suggestion of an unannounced descent on Cannes, and persuaded her to follow his example and inform her lover that she would await news from him in Paris. They were to put up at the European, and telegrams there from Cannes would find them on and after April 28th. All this valuable information was contained in the despatches, which lay, with their priceless messages, on the said April 28th, in Mr. Arthur Laing's flannel jacket, inside his portmanteau, on the way to Paris.

Paris claims to be the centre of the world, and if it be, the world has a very good centre. Anyhow Paris becomes, from this moment, the centre of this drama. Not only was Arthur Laing being whirled there by the Nice express, and Miss Bussey's party proceeding thither by the eleven o'clock train from Victoria—Mary laughed as she thought it might have been her honeymoon she was starting on—but the Bellairs and their friends were heading for the same point. Miss Bussey's party had the pleasanter journey; they were all of one mind; Miss Bussey was eager to reach Paris because it was the end of the journey; John and Mary desired nothing but the moment when with trembling fingers they should tear open their telegrams in the hall of the hotel. The expedition from the south did not enjoy a like unanimity; but before following their steps we may, in the interest of simplicity, land the first detachment safely at its destination.

When Mary and John, followed by Miss Bussey—they outstripped her in their eagerness—entered the hotel, a young man with an eye-glass was just engaging a bedroom. John took his place beside the stranger, and asked in a voice, which he strove to render calm, if there were any letters for——

"Beg pardon, sir. In one moment," said the clerk, and he added to Laing, "Number 37, sir." Laing—O irony of things!—turned on John and his companion just that one supercilious glance which we bestow on other tourists, and followed his baggage upstairs.

"Anything," resumed John, "for Miss Travers or Mr. Ashforth?" And he succeeded in looking as if he did not care a straw whether there were or not.

After a search the porter answered,

"Nothing, sir."

"What?" exclaimed John, aghast. "Oh, nonsense, look again."

Another search followed; it was without result.

John saw Mary's appealing eyes fixed on him.

"Nothing," he said tragically.

"Oh, John!"

"Have you taken the rooms, John?" inquired Miss Bussey impatiently.

"No. I'm sorry. I forgot all about them."

Miss Bussey was tired; she had been sea-sick, and the train always made her feel queer.

"Has neither of you got an ounce of wits about you?" she demanded, and plunged forward to the desk. John and Mary received their numbers in gloomy silence, and mounted the stairs.

Now Arthur Laing, in his hasty survey of the party, had arrived at a not unnatural but wholly erroneous conclusion. He had seen a young man, rather nervous, a young woman, looking anxious and shy, and an elderly person, plainly dressed (Miss Bussey was no dandy) sitting (Miss Bussey always sat as soon as she could) on a trunk. He took John and Mary for a newly-married couple, and Miss Bussey for an old family servant, detailed to look after her young mistress's entry into independent housekeeping.

"More infernal honeymooners," he said to himself, as he washed his hands. "The place is always full of 'em. Girl wasn't bad-looking, though."

The next morning, unhappily, confirmed him in his mistake. For Miss Bussey, overcome by the various trials of the day before, kept her bed, and when Laing came down, the first sight which met his eyes was a breakfast-table, whereat Mary and John sat *tête-à-tête.* He eyed them with that mixture of scorn and envy which their supposed situation awakens in a bachelor's heart, and took a place from which he could survey them at leisure. There is a bright side to everything, and that of Laing's mistake was the pleasure he derived from his delusion. Sticking his glass firmly in his eye, he watched like a cat for those playful little endearments which his cynical mood—he was, like many of us, not at his best in the morning—led him to anticipate. He watched in vain. The young people were decorum itself; more than that, they showed signs of preoccupation; they spoke only occasionally, and then with a business-like brevity.

Suddenly the waiter entered with a handful of letters, which he proceeded to distribute. Laing expected none, and kept his gaze on his honeymooners. To his surprise they showed animation enough now; their eyes were fixed on the waiter's approaching form;

the bridegroom even rose an inch or two from his seat; both stretched out their hands.

Alas, with a little bow, a smile, and a shrug, the waiter passed by, and the disappointed couple sank back, with looks of blank despair.

Surely here was enough to set any open-minded man on the right track! Yes; but not enough to free one who was tied and bound to his own theory.

" She's dashed anxious to hear from home," mused Laing. " Poor girl! It ain't over and above flattering to him, though."

He finished his breakfast, and went out to smoke. Presently he saw his friends come out also; they went to the porter's desk, and he heard one of them say " telegram." A sudden idea struck him.

" I am an ass!" said he. " Tell you what it is; they've wired for rooms somewhere— Monte, most likely—and can't start till they get an answer."

He was so pleased with his explanation that his last doubt vanished, and he watched Mary and John start for a walk—the fraternal relations they had established would have allowed such a thing even in London, much more in Paris—with a most benevolent smile.

"Aunt Sarah is really quite poorly," remarked Mary, as they crossed the road and entered the Tuileries Gardens. "She'll have to stay in all to-day and perhaps to-morrow. Isn't it hard on her? Paris amuses her so much."

John expressed his sympathy.

"Now, if it had been you or I," he ended, "we shouldn't have minded. Paris doesn't amuse us just now."

"Oh, but, John, we must be ready to start at any moment."

"*You* can't start without Miss Bussey."

"I think that in a *wagon-lit*——" began Mary.

"But what's the good of talking?" cried John bitterly. "Why is there no news from her?"

"He *might* have wired. John, is it possible our telegrams went astray?"

"Well, we must wait a day or two; or, if you like, we can wire again."

Mary hesitated.

"I—I can't do that, John. Suppose he'd received the first, and—and——"

"Yes, I see. I don't want to humiliate myself either."

"We'll wait a day, anyhow. And, now,

John, let's think no more about them! Oh, well, that's nonsense; but let's enjoy ourselves as well as we can."

They managed to enjoy themselves very well. The town was new to Mary, and John found a pleasure in showing it off to her. After a morning of sight-seeing, they drove in the Bois, and ended the day at the theatre. Miss Bussey, unfortunately, was no better. She had sent for an English doctor, and he talked vaguely about two or three days in bed. Mary ventured to ask whether her aunt could travel.

" Oh, if absolutely necessary, perhaps; but much better not," was the answer.

Well, it was not absolutely necessary yet, for no letter and no telegram arrived. This was the awful fact that greeted them when they came in from the theatre.

"We'll wire the first thing to-morrow," declared John in a resolute tone. " Write yours to-night, Mary, and I'll give them to the porter——"

" Oh, not mine, please," cried Mary in shrinking bashfulness. " I can't let the porter see mine ! "

" Well, then, we'll take them out before breakfast to-morrow."

F

To this Mary agreed; and they sat down and wrote their despatches. While they were so engaged, Laing jumped out of a cab and entered the room. He seized an English paper, and, flinging himself into a chair, began to study the sporting news. Presently he stole a glance at Mary. It so chanced that just at the same moment she was stealing a glance at him. Mary dropped her eyes with a blush; Laing withdrew behind his paper.

"Shy, of course. Anybody would be," he thought, with a smile.

"Did you like the piece, Mary?" asked John.

"Oh, very much. I wish Aunt Sarah could have seen it. She missed so much fun."

"Well, she could hardly have come with us, could she?" remarked John.

"Oh no," said Mary.

"Well, I should rather think not," whispered Laing, who failed to identify "Aunt Sarah" with the elderly person on the trunk.

"I shouldn't have been happy if she had," said Mary.

"I simply wouldn't have let her," said John in that authoritative tone which so well became him.

" No more would I in your place, old chap,'' murmured Mr. Laing.

Mary rose.

" Thanks for all your kindness, John. Good night.''

"I'm so glad you've had a pleasant day. Good night, Mary.''

So they parted—with a good night as calm, as decorous, as frankly fraternal as one could wish (or wish otherwise). Yet its very virtues undid it in the prematurely suspicious eyes of Arthur Laing. For no sooner was he left alone than he threw down his paper and began to chuckle.

" All for my benefit, that, eh ? Good night, Mary ! Good night, John ! Lord ! Lord !'' and he rose, lit a cigarette, and ordered a brandy and soda. And ever and again he smiled. He felt very acute.

So vain is it for either wisdom or simplicity, candour or diplomacy—nay, for facts themselves—to struggle against a Man with a Theory. Mr. Laing went to bed, no more doubting that Mary and John were man and wife, than he doubted that he had " spotted '' the winner of the Derby. Certitude could no farther go.

CHAPTER VII.

THE SIGHTS OF AVIGNON.

"It's a curious thing," observed Roger Deane, "but this fellow Baedeker always travels the opposite way to what I do. When I'm coming back, he's always going out, and *vice versa*. It makes him precious difficult to understand, I can tell you, Miss Dora. However, I think I've got him now. Listen to this. 'Marseilles to Arles (Amphitheatre starred) one day. Arles to Avignon (Palace of the Popes starred) two days—slow going that—Avignon to——'"

"Do you want to *squat* in this wretched country, Sir Roger?" demanded Dora angrily.

A faint smile played round Sir Roger's lips.

"You're the only one who's in a hurry," he remarked.

"No, I'm not. Mr. Ellerton is in just as much of a hurry."

" Then he bears disappointment better."

" What in the world did papa and—well, and Lady Deane, you know—want to stop here for ? "

" You don't seem to understand how interesting Marseilles is. Let me read you a passage : ' Marseilles was a colony founded about 600 B.C.' — What ? Oh, all right ! We'll skip a bit. ' In 1792 hordes of galley-slaves were sent hence to Paris, where they committed frightful excesses.' That's what Maud and your father are going to do. ' It was for them that Rouget—— ' I say, what's the matter, Miss Dora ? "

" I don't know why you should enjoy teasing me, but you *have* nearly made me cry, so perhaps you'll be happy now."

" You tried to take me in. I pretended to be taken in. That's all."

" Well, it was very unkind of you."

" So, after all, it's not a matter of indifference to you at what rate we travel, as you said in the train to-day ? "

" Oh, I had to. I—I couldn't let papa see."

" And why are you in a hurry ? "

" I can't tell you ; but I must—oh, I must ! —be in England in four days."

" You'll hardly get your father to give up a day at Avignon."

" Well, one day there ; then we should just do it, if we only slept in Paris."

" Yes, but my wife—— "

" Oh, you can stay. Don't say anything about Paris yet. Help me to get there. I'll make papa go on. Please do, Sir Roger. I shall be so awfully obliged to you; so will Mr. Ellerton."

" Charlie Ellerton? Not he! He's in no hurry."

" What do you mean? Didn't you hear him to-day urging papa to travel straight through ? "

" Oh, yes, I heard that."

" Well ? "

" You were there then."

" What of that ? "

" He's not so pressing when you're away."

" I don't understand. Why should he pretend to be in a hurry when he isn't ? "

" Ah, I don't know. Don't you ? "

" Not in the least, Sir Roger. But never mind Mr. Ellerton. Will you help me ? "

" As far as Paris. You must look out for yourself there."

These terms Dora accepted. Surely at

Paris she would hear some news of or from John Ashforth. She thought he must have written one line in response to her last letter, and that his answer must have been so far delayed as to arrive at Cannes after her departure; it would be waiting for her at Paris and would tell her whether she was in time or whether there was no more use in hurrying. The dread that oppressed her was lest, arriving too late in Paris, she should find that she had missed happiness by reason of this wretched dawdling in Southern France.

Seeing her meditative, Deane slipped away to his cigar, and she sat in the hotel hall, musing. Deane's revelation of Charlie's treachery hardly surprised her; she meant to upbraid him severely, but she was conscious that, if little surprised, she was hardly more than a little angry. His conduct was indeed contemptible, it revealed an utter instability and fickleness of mind which made her gravely uneasy as to Mary Travers's chances of permanent happiness. Yes, scornful one might be; but who could be seriously angry with the poor boy? And perhaps, after all, she did him injustice. Some natures were more prone than others to sudden passions; it really did not follow that a feeling must be either shallow or short-lived because it was sudden; whether it survived or passed away would depend chiefly on the person who excited it.   Clearly Mary Travers was incapable of maintaining a permanent hold over Charlie's affections, but another girl might be—might have been more successful. It would perhaps be a pity if Charlie and Mary Travers were to come together again. Were they really suited to one another? She pictured Mary as a severe, rather stern young woman; and she hardly knew whether to laugh or groan at the thought of Charlie adapting himself to such a mate.   Meanwhile her own position was certainly very difficult, and she acknowledged its thorniness with a little sigh.   To begin with, the suspense was terrible; at times she would have been almost relieved to hear that John was married beyond recall. Then Charlie was a great and a growing difficulty.   He had not actually repeated the passionate indiscretion of which he had been guilty at Cannes, but more and more watchfulness and severity were needed to keep him within the bounds proper to their relative positions; and it was odious to be disagreeable to a fellow-traveller, especially when he was such a good and devoted friend as Charlie.

Sir Roger loyally carried out his bargain. Lady Deane was hurried on, leaving Marseilles, with its varied types of humanity and its profound social significance, practically unexplored : Arles and Amphitheatre, in spite of the beckoning " star," were dropped out of the programme, and the next day found the party at Avignon. Now they were once more for a moment in harmony. Dora could spare twenty-four hours ; Lady Deane and the General were mollified by conscious unselfishness ; the prospect of a fresh struggle at Paris lay well in the background and was discreetly ignored ; Charlie Ellerton, who had reached the most desperate stage of love, looked neither back nor forward. It was enough for him to have wrung four and twenty hours of Dora's company from fate's reluctant grasp. He meant to make the most of them.

She and he sat, on the afternoon of their arrival, in the gardens, hard by the Cathedral, where Lady Deane and the General were doing their duty. Sir Roger had chartered a cab and gone for a drive on the boulevards.

" And we shall really be in Paris to-morrow night ? " said Dora. " And in England, I hope, six and thirty hours afterwards ! I want papa to cross the next evening. Mr. Ellerton, I believe we shall be in time."

Charlie said nothing. He seemed to be engrossed by the magnificent view before him.

"Well? Have you nothing to say?" she asked. ·

"It's a sin to rush through a place like this," he observed. "We ought to stay a week. There's no end to see. It's an education!"

By way, probably, of making the most of his brief opportunity, he went on gazing, across the river which flowed below, now toward the heights of Mont Ventoux, now at the ramparts of Villeneuve. Dora, on the other hand, fixed pensive eyes on his curly hatless head, which leant forward as he rested his elbows on his knees. He had referred to the attractions of Avignon in tones of almost overpowering emotion.

Presently he turned his head towards her with a quick jerk.

"I don't want to be in time," he said; and, with equal rapidity, he returned to his survey of Villeneuve.

Dora made no answer, unless a perplexed wrinkle on her brow might serve for one. A long silence followed. It was broken at last by Charlie. He left the landscape, with a sigh of satisfaction, as though he could not reproach himself with having neglected it, and directed his gaze into his companion's eyes. Dora blushed and pulled the brim of her hat a little lower down on her forehead.

"What's more," said Charlie in deliberate tones, as if no pause had occurred between this remark and his last, "I don't believe you do."

Dora started and straightened herself in her seat; it looked as if the rash remark were to be met with a burst of indignation, but, a second later, she leant back again and smiled scornfully.

"How can you be so silly, Mr. Ellerton?" she asked.

"We both of us," pursued Charlie, "see now that we made up our minds to be very foolish; we both of us mistook our real feelings; we're beginning—at least I began some time ago, and you're beginning now—to understand the true state of affairs."

"Oh, I know what you mean, and I ought to be very angry, I suppose; but it's too absurd."

"Not in the least. The absurd thing is

your fancying that you care about this fellow Ashforth."

"No, you must really stop, you must indeed. I don't——"

"I know the sort of fellow he is—a dull, dry chap, who makes love as if he was dancing a minuet."

"You're quite wrong."

"And kisses you as if it was part of the church service."

This last description, applied to John Ashforth's manner of wooing, had enough of aptness to stir Dora into genuine resentment.

"A girl doesn't like a man less because he respects her; nor more because he ridicules better men than himself."

"Don't be angry. I'm only saying what's true. Why should I want to run him down?"

"I suppose—well, I suppose because——"

"Well?"

"You're a little bit—but I don't think I ought to talk about it."

"Jealous, you were going to say."

"Was I?"

"And that shows you know what I mean."

"Well, by now I suppose I do. I can't help your doing it or I would."

Charlie moved closer, and leaning forward

till his face was only a yard from hers, while his hand, sliding along the back of the seat, almost touched her, said in a low voice,

" Are you sure you would ? "

Dora's answer was a laugh—a laugh with a hint of nervousness in it. Perhaps she knew what was in it, for she looked away towards the river.

" Dolly," he whispered, " shall I go back to Cannes ? Shall I ? "

Perhaps the audacity of this *per saltum* advance from the distance of " Miss Bellairs " to the ineffable assumption involved in " Dolly " made the subject of it dumb.

" I will, if you ask me," he said, as she was silent for a space.

Then, with profile towards him and eyes away, she murmured,

" What would Miss Travers say if you turned back now ? "

The mention of Mary did not on this occasion evoke any unseemly words. On the contrary, Charlie smiled. He glanced at his companion. He glanced behind him and round him. Then, drilling his deep design into the semblance of an uncontrollable impulse, he seized Dora's hand in his and, before she could stir, kissed her cheek.

She leapt to her feet.

" How dare you ? " she cried.

" How could I help it ? "

" I'll never speak to you again.   No gentleman would have—oh, I do hope you're ashamed of yourself ! "

Her words evidently struck home.   With an air of contrition he sank on the seat.

" I'm a beast," he said ruefully.   " You're quite right, Miss Bellairs. Don't have anything more to say to me. I wish I was—I wish I had some—some self-control—and self-respect, you know. If I were a fellow like Ashforth now, I should never have done that ! Of course you can't forgive me ; " and, in his extremity of remorse, he buried his face in his hands.

Dora stood beside him.   She made one step as if to leave him ; a glance at him brought her back, and she looked down at him for a minute.   Presently a troubled, doubtful little smile appeared on her face ; when she realized it was there, she promptly banished it. Alas ! It was too late. The rascal had been peeping through his fingers, and, with a ringing laugh, he sprang to his feet, caught both her hands, and cried,

" Shocking, wasn't it ?   Awful ? "

" Let me go, Mr. Ellerton."

" Must I ? "

" Yes, yes."

" Why ? Why, when you——? "

" Sir Roger's coming. Look behind you."

" Oh, the deuce ! "

An instant later they were sitting demurely at opposite ends of the seat, inspecting Villeneuve with interest.

In another moment Deane stood before them, puffing a cigarette and wearing an expression of amiability tempered by boredom.

" Wonderful old place, isn't it, Deane ? " asked Charlie.

" Such a view, Sir Roger ! " cried Dora, in almost breathless enthusiasm.

" You certainly," assented Deane, "do see some wonderful sights on this promenade. I'm glad I came up. The air's given you quite a colour, Miss Dora."

" It's tea-time," declared Dora suddenly. " Take me down with you, Sir Roger. Mr. Ellerton, go and tell the others we're going home to tea."

Charlie started off, and Sir Roger strolled along by Miss Bellairs's side. Presently he said,

" Still anxious to get to Paris ? "

"Why shouldn't I be?" she asked quickly.

"I thought perhaps the charms of Avignon would have decided you to linger. Haven't you been tempted?"

Dora glanced at him, but his face betrayed no secondary meaning.

"Tempted? Oh, perhaps," she answered, with the same nervous little laugh, "but not quite led astray. I'm going on."

CHAPTER VIII.

MR. AND MRS. ASHFORTH (1).

ALL that evening Miss Bellairs was not observed—and Deane watched her very closely —to address a word to Charlie Ellerton; even "good night" was avoided by a premature disappearance and unexpected failure to return. Perhaps it was part of the same policy of seclusion which made her persuade Lady Deane to travel to Paris with her in one compartment and relegate the men to another—a proposal which the banished accepted by an enthusiastic majority of two to one. The General foresaw an infinity of quiet naps and Deane uninterrupted smoking; Charlie alone chafed against the necessary interruption of his bold campaign, but, in face of Dora's calm coldness of aspect, he did not dare to lift up his voice.

Lady Deane was so engrossed in the study —or the search for opportunities of study—of sides of life with which she was unfamiliar as to be, for the most part, blind to what took place immediately around her. General Bellairs himself (who vaguely supposed that some man might try to make love to his daughter five years hence, and thereupon be promptly sent off with a flea in his ear) was not more unconscious than she that there was, had been, or might be anything, as the phrase runs, " between " the two junior members of the party. Lady Deane had no hints to give and no questions to ask ; she seated herself placidly in a corner and began to write in a large note-book. She had been unwillingly compelled to " scamp " Marseilles, but, as she wrote, she found that the rough notes she was copying, aided by fresh memory, supplied her with an ample fund of material. Alternately she smiled contentedly to herself, and gazed out of the window with a preoccupied air. Clearly a plot was brewing, and the author was grateful to Dora for restricting her interruptions to an occasional impatient sigh and the taking up and dropping again of her Tauchnitz.

With the men tongues moved more.

" Well, General," said Deane, " what's Miss Dora's *ultimatum* about your staying in Paris ? "

Charlie pricked up his ears and buried his face behind *La Vie Parisienne.*

"You'll think me very weak, Deane," rejoined the General with an apologetic laugh, "but I've promised to go straight on if she wants me to."

"And does she?"

"I don't know what the child has got in her head, but she says she'll tell me when she gets to Paris. We shall have a day with you anyhow; I don't think she's so set on not staying as she was, but I don't profess to understand her fancies. Still, as you see, I yield to them."

"Man's task in the world," said Deane. "Eh, Charlie? What are you hiding behind that paper for?"

"I was only looking at the pictures."

"Quite enough too. You're going to stay in Paris, aren't you?"

"Don't know yet, old fellow. It depends on whether I get a letter calling me back or not."

"Hang it, one might as well be in a house where the shooting turns out a fraud. Nobody knows that he won't have a wire any morning and have to go back to town. My wife'll be furious if you desert her, General."

"Oh, I hope it won't come to that."

"I hope awfully that I shall be able to stay," said Charlie with obvious sincerity.

"Then," observed Deane with a slight smile, "if the General and Miss Bellairs leave us you can take my wife about."

"I should think you might take her yourself;" and he kicked Deane gently. He was afraid of arousing the General's dormant suspicions.

It was late at night when they arrived in Paris, but the faithful Laing was on the platform to meet them, and received them with a warm greeting. While the luggage was being collected by Deane's man, they stood and talked on the platform. Presently the General, struck by a sudden thought, asked,

"I suppose nothing came for us at Cannes, eh, Laing? You said you'd bring anything on, you know."

Laing interrupted a pretty speech which he was trying to direct into Dora's inattentive ears.

"Beg pardon, General?"

"No letters for any of us before you left Cannes?"

"No, Gen——" he began, but suddenly

stopped. His mouth remained open and his glass fell from his eye.

The General, not waiting to hear more than the first word, had rushed off to hail a cab, and Deane was escorting his wife. Dora and Charlie stood waiting for the unfinished speech.

The end came slowly and with a prodigious emphasis of despair.

" Oh, by Jove ! "

" Well, Mr. Laing ? " said Dora.

" The morning you left—just after—there were two telegrams."

" For me ? " cried each of his auditors.

" One for each of you, but—— "

" Oh, give me mine."

" Hand over mine, old chap."

" I—I haven't got 'em."

" What ? "

" I—I'm awfully sorry, I—I forgot 'em."

" Oh, how tiresome of you, Mr. Laing ! "

" Send 'em round first thing to-morrow, Laing."

" But—but I don't know where I put 'em. I know I laid 'em down. Then I took 'em up. Then I put 'em—where the deuce did I put 'em ? Here's a go, Miss Bellairs ! I say, I am an ass ! "

No contradiction assailed him. His victims glared reproachfully at him.

"I must have left them at Cannes. I'll wire first thing in the morning, Miss Bellairs; I'll get up as soon as ever the office is open. I say, do forgive me."

"Well, Mr. Laing, I'll try, but—— "

"Laing! Here! My wife wants you," shouted Sir Roger; and the criminal, happy to escape, ran away, leaving Dora and Charlie alone.

"They must have been from *them*," murmured Dora.

"No doubt; and that fool Laing—— "

"What has he done with them?"

"Lit his pipe with them, I expect."

"Oh, what shall we do?"

"I don't know."

"What—what do you think they said, Mr. Ellerton?"

"How can I tell? Perhaps that the marriage was off!"

"Oh!" escaped from Dora.

"Perhaps that it was going on."

"It's worse than ever. They may have asked for answers."

"Probably."

"And they won't have written here!"

" Sure not to have."

" And—and I shan't know what to do. I —I believe it was to say he had broken off the marriage."

" Is the wish father to the thought ? "

The lights of the station flickered, but Charlie saw, or thought he saw, a hasty, unpremeditated gesture of protest.

" Dolly ! " he whispered.

" Hush, hush ! How can you now—before we know ? "

" The cab's waiting," called Deane. "Come along."

They got in in silence. The General and the Deanes went first, and the three young people followed in a second vehicle. It was but just twelve, and the boulevards were gay and full of people.

Suddenly, as they were near the Opera, they saw the tall figure of an unmistakable Englishman walking away from them down the Avenue de l'Opéra. Dora clutched Charlie's arm with a convulsive grip.

" Hallo, what's the—— ? " he began ; but a second pinch enforced silence.

" See that chap ? " asked Laing, pointing to the figure. " He's at my hotel."

" Is he ? " said Dora in a faint voice,

"Yes; I've got a good deal of amusement out of him. He oughtn't to be out so late though, and by himself, too!"

"Who is it?" asked Charlie.

"I don't know his name."

"And why oughtn't he to be out?"

"Because he's on his honeymoon."

"What?" cried Dora.

"Just married," explained Laing. "Wife's a tallish girl, fair, rather good-looking; looks standoffish though."

"You—you're sure they're married, Mr. Laing?" gasped Dora; and Charlie, in whom her manner had awakened a suspicion of the truth, also waited eagerly for the reply.

"What, Miss Bellairs?" asked Laing in surprise.

"Oh, I mean—I mean you haven't made a mistake?"

"Well, they're together all day, and nobody's with them except a lady's-maid. I should think that's good enough."

With a sigh Dora sank back against the cushions. They were at the hotel now; the others had already entered, and, bidding Laing a hearty good-night, Dora ran in, followed closely by Charlie. He did not overtake her before she found her father.

" Well, Dolly," said the General, " there's no letter."

" Oh," cried Dolly, " I'll stay as long as ever you like, papa."

" That's right," said Deane. " And you, Charlie ? "

Charlie took his cue.

" A month if you like."

" Capital ! Now for a wash—come along, Maud—and then supper ! "

Dora lingered behind the others, and Charlie with her. Directly they were alone, he asked,

" What does it all mean ? "

She sat down, still panting with agitation.

" Why—why, that man we saw—the man Mr. Laing says is on his honeymoon, is—is—— "

" Yes, yes ? "

" Mr. Ashforth ! "

" Dolly ! And his wife ! By Jove ! It's an exact description of Mary Travers ! "

" The telegrams were to say the marriage was to be at once."

" Yes, and—they're married ! "

" Yes ! "

A short pause marked the astounding conclusion. Then Charlie came up very close and whispered,

" Are you broken-hearted, Dolly ? "

She turned her face away with a blush.

" Are you, Dolly ? "

" I'm very much ashamed of myself," she murmured. " Oh, Mr. Ellerton, not just yet!" And in deference to her entreaty Charlie had the grace to postpone what he was about to do.

When the supper was ready, Sir Roger Deane looked round the table inquiringly.

" Well," said he, " what is it to be ? "

" Champagne—champagne in magnums ! " cried Charlie Ellerton with a triumphant laugh.

CHAPTER IX.

MR. AND MRS. ASHFORTH (2).

Miss Bussey was much relieved when the doctor pronounced her convalescent, and allowed her to come downstairs. To fall ill on an outing is always exasperating, but beyond that she felt that her enforced seclusion was particularly unfortunate at the moment. Here were two young people, not engaged nor going to be engaged to one another; and for three days or more circumstances had abandoned them to an inevitable and unchaperoned *tête-à-tête!* Mary made light of it; she relied on the fraternal relationship; but that was, after all, a fiction, quite incapable, in Miss Bussey's opinion, of supporting the strain to which it had been subjected. Besides, Mary's sincerity appeared doubtful; the kind girl, anxious to spare her aunt worry, minimised the difficulties of her position; but Miss Bussey detected a restlessness in her manner which clearly betrayed uneasiness. Here, of course, Miss Bussey was wrong; neither Mary nor John were the least self-conscious; they felt no embarrassment, but, poor creatures, wore out their spirits in a useless vigil over the letter-rack.

Miss Bussey was restored to active life on the morning after the party from Cannes arrived in Paris, and she hastened to emphasise the fact of her return to complete health by the unusual effort of coming down to breakfast. She was in high feather, and her cheery conversation lifted, to some extent, the gloom which had settled on her young friends. While exhorting to patience, she was full of hope, and dismissed as chimerical all the darker explanations which the disconsolate lovers invented to account for the silence their communications had met with. Under her influence the breakfast-table became positively cheerful, and at last all the three burst into a hearty laugh at one of the old lady's little jokes.

At this moment Arthur Laing entered the room. His brow was clouded. He had searched his purse, his cigar-case, the lining of his hat—in fact, every depository where a careful man would be likely to bestow documents whose existence he wished to remember; as no careful man would put such things in the pocket of his "blazer," he had not searched there; thus the telegrams had not appeared, and the culprit was looking forward, with some alarm, to the reception which would await him when he "turned up" to lunch with his friends, as he had promised to do. Hardly, however, had he sat down to his coffee when his sombre thoughts were cleared away by the extraordinary spectacle of young Mr. and Mrs. Ashforth hobnobbing with their maid, the latter lady appearing quite at home and leading the gaiety and the conversation. Laing laid down his roll and his knife and looked at them in undisguised amazement.

For a moment doubt of his cherished theory began to assail his mind. He heard the old lady call Ashforth "John"; that was a little strange; and it was rather strange that John answered by saying: "That must be as you wish; I am entirely at your disposal." And yet, reflected Laing, was it very strange, after all? In his own family they had an old retainer who called all the children, whatever their age, by their Christian names, and was admitted to a degree of intimacy hardly distinguishable from that accorded to a relative.

Laing, weighing the evidence *pro* and *contra*, decided that there was an overwhelming balance in favour of his old view, and dismissed the matter with the comment that, if it ever befell him to go on a wedding-tour, he would ask his wife to take a maid with rather less claims on her kindness and his toleration.

That same morning the second pair of telegrams, forwarded by post from Cannes, duly arrived. Dora and Charlie, reading them in the light of their recent happy information, found them most kind and comforting, although in reality they, apart from their missing forerunners, told the recipients nothing at all. John's ran: "Am in Paris at European. Please write. Anxious to hear. Everything decided for the best.—JOHN." Mary's to Charlie was even briefer; it said: "Am here at European. Why no answer to last?"

"It's really very kind of Mr. Ashforth," said Dora to Charlie, as they strolled in the garden of the Tuileries, "to make such a point of what I think. I expect the wire that stupid Mr. Laing lost was just to tell me the date of the marriage."

"Not a doubt of it. Miss Tr—Mrs. Ash-forth's wire to me makes that clear. They want to hear that we're not desperately unhappy. Well, we aren't, are we, Dolly?"

"Well, perhaps not."

"Isn't it extraordinary how we mistook our feelings? Of course, though, it's natural in you. You had never been through any-thing of the sort before. How could you tell whether it was the real thing or not?"

Dora shot a glance out of the corner of her eye at her lover, but did not disclaim the innocence he imputed to her; she knew men liked to think that, and why shouldn't they, poor things? She seized on his implied ad-mission, and carried the war into his country.

"But you—you who are so experienced—how did you come to make such a mistake?"

Charlie was not at a loss.

"It wasn't a mistake *then*," he said. "I was quite right then. Mary Travers was about the nicest girl I had ever seen. I thought her as charming as a girl could be."

"Oh, you did! Then why——"

"My eyes have been opened since then."

"What did that?"

"Why don't you ever pronounce my name?"

"Never mind your name. What opened your eyes?"

"Why, yours, of course."

"What nonsense! They're very nice about it, aren't they? Do you think we ought to call?"

"Shall you feel it awkward?"

"Yes, a little. Shan't you? Still we must let them know we're here. Will you write to Mrs. Ashforth?"

"I suppose I'd better. After lunch 'll do, won't it?"

"Oh, yes. And I'll write a note to him. I expect they won't be staying here long."

"I hope not. Hallo, it's a quarter past twelve. We must be getting back. Laing's coming to lunch."

"Where are the Deanes?"

"Lady Deane's gone to Belleville with your father to see slums, and Roger's playing tennis with Laing. He said we weren't to wait lunch. Are you hungry, Dolly?"

"Not very. It seems only an hour since breakfast."

"How charming of you! We've been walking here since ten o'clock."

"Mr. Ellerton, will you be serious for a minute? I want to say something important.

When we meet the Ashforths there mustn't be a word said about—about—you know."

" Why not ? "

" Oh, I couldn't ! So soon ! Surely you see that. Why, it would be hardly civil to them, would it, apart from anything else ? "

" Well, it might look rather casual."

" And I positively couldn't face John Ashforth. You promise, don't you ? "

" It's a nuisance, because, you see, Dolly—— "

" You're not to get into the habit of saying ' Dolly.' At least not yet."

" Presently ? "

" If you're good. Now promise ! "

" All right."

" We're not engaged."

" All right."

" Nor thinking of it."

" Rather not ! "

" That's very nice of you, and when the Ashforths are gone—— "

" I shall be duly rewarded ? "

" Oh, we'll see. Do come along. Papa hates being kept waiting for his meals, and they must have finished their slums long ago."

They found Lady Deane and the General

waiting for them, and the latter proposed an adjournment to a famous restaurant near the Opera. Thither they repaired, and ordered their lunch.

"Deane and Laing will find out where we've gone and follow," said the General. "We won't wait," and he resumed his conversation with Lady Deane on the events of the morning.

A moment later the absentees came in; Sir Roger in his usual leisurely fashion, Laing hurriedly. The latter held in his hand two telegrams, or the crumpled *débris* thereof. He rushed up to the table, and panted out, "Found 'em in the pocket of my blazer— must have put 'em there—stupid ass—never thought of it—put it on for tennis—awfully sorry."

Wasting no time in reproaches, Dora and Charlie grasped their recovered property.

"Excuse me!" they cried simultaneously, and opened the envelopes. A moment later both leant back in their chairs, pictures of helpless bewilderment.

Dora had read: "Marriage broken off. Coming to you 28th. Write directions— European, Paris."

Charlie had read: "Engagement at end.

Aunt and I coming to Paris—European, on 28th. Can you meet?"

Lady Deane was writing in her notebook. The General, Sir Roger, and Laing were busy with the waiter, the *menu*, and the wine-list. Quick as thought the lovers exchanged telegrams. They read, and looked at one another.

"What does it mean?" whispered Dora.

"You never saw anything like the lives those ragpickers lead, Dora," observed Lady Deane, looking up from her task. "I was talking to one this morning, and he said——"

"Maitre d'hôtel for me," broke in Sir Roger.

"I haven't a notion," murmured Charlie.

"Look here, what's your liquor, Laing?"

"Anything; with this thirst on me——"

"There are ample materials for a revolution more astonishing and sanguinary——"

"Nonsense, General, you must have something to drink."

"Can they have changed their minds again, Dolly?"

"They must have, if Mr. Laing is——"

"Dry? I should think I was. So would you be, if you'd been playing tennis."

Laing cut across the currents of conversation.

"Hope no harm done, Miss Bellairs, about that wire?"

"I—I—I don't think so."

"Or yours, Charlie?"

Charlie took a hopeful view.

"Upon my honour, Laing, I'm glad you hid it."

"Oh, I see!" cried Laing. "Tip for the wrong 'un, eh, and too late to put it on now?"

"You're not far off," answered Charlie Ellerton.

"Roger, is it to-night that the General is going to take me to the——?"

"Hush! Not before Miss Bellairs, my dear! Consider her filial feelings. You and the General must make a quiet bolt of it. *We're* only going to the *Palais Royal.*"

The arrival of fish brought a momentary pause, but the first mouthful was hardly swallowed when Arthur Laing started, hunted hastily for his eyeglass, and stuck it in his eye.

"Yes, it is them," said he. "See, Charlie, that table over there! They've got their backs to us, but I can see 'em in the mirror."

"See who?" asked Charlie in an irritable tone.

" Why, those honeymooners. I say, Lady Deane, it's a queer thing to have a lady's-maid to breakf—— Why, by Jove, she's with them now! Look!"

His excited interest aroused the attention of the whole party, and they looked across the long room.

"Ashforth's their name," concluded Laing. "I heard the Abigail call him Ashforth; and the lady is——"

He was interrupted by the clatter of a knife and fork falling on a plate. He turned in the direction whence the sound came.

Dora Bellairs leant back in her chair, her hands in her lap; Charlie Ellerton had hidden himself behind the wine-list. Lady Deane, her husband, and the General gazed inquiringly at Dora.

At the same instant there came a shrill little cry from the other end of the room. The mirror had served Mary Travers as well as it had Laing. For a moment she spoke hastily to her companions; then she and John rose, and, with radiant smiles on their faces, advanced towards their friends. The long expected meeting had come at last.

Dora sat still in consternation. Charlie,

peeping out from behind his *menu*, saw the approach.

"Now, in heaven's name," he groaned, " are they married or aren't they?" and, having said this, he awaited the worst.

CHAPTER X.

MR. AND NOT MRS. ASHFORTH.

Suum cuique: to the Man belongeth courage in great things, but in affairs of small moment Woman is pre-eminent. Charlie Ellerton was speechless; Dora Bellairs, by a supreme effort, rose on shaking legs and advanced with out-stretched hands to meet John Ashforth.

"Mr. Ashforth, I declare! Who would have thought of meeting you here?" she exclaimed; and she added, in an almost imperceptible mysterious whisper, "Hush!"

John at once understood that he was to make no reference to the communications which had resulted in this happy meeting. He expressed a friendly gratification in appropriate words. Dora began to breathe again; everything was passing off well. Suddenly she glanced from John to Mary. Mary stood alone, about three yards from the table, gazing at Charlie. Charlie sat as though paralysed. He would ruin everything.

"Mr. Ellerton," she called sharply. Charlie started up, but before he could reach Dora's side, the latter had turned to Mary and was holding out a friendly hand. Mary responded with alacrity.

"Miss Bellairs, isn't it? We ought to know one another. I'm so glad to meet you."

Charlie was by them now.

"And how do you do, Mr. Ellerton?" went on Mary, rivalling Dora in composure. And she also added a barely visible and quite inaudible "Hush!"

"Who are they?" asked Deane in a low voice.

"Their name's Ashforth," answered Laing.

"God bless my soul!" exclaimed the General. "I remember him now. We made his acquaintance at Interlaken, but his name had slipped from my memory. And that's his wife? Fine girl, too. I must speak to him." And, full of kindly intent, he bustled off and shook John warmly by the hand.

"My dear Ashforth, delighted to meet you again, and under such delightful conditions, too! Ah, well, it only comes once in a lifetime, does it?—in your case anyhow, I hope.

I see Dora has introduced herself. You must present me. When was it?"

Portions of this address puzzled John considerably, but he thought it best to do as he was told.

"Mary," he said, "let me introduce General Bellairs—Miss Bellairs's father—to you. General Bell—— "

The General interrupted him by addressing Mary with much effusion.

"Delighted to meet you. Ah, you know our young friend Ellerton? Everybody does, it seems to me. Come, you must join us. Waiter, two more places. Lady Deane, let me introduce Mrs. Ashforth. They're on their—— "

He paused. An inarticulate sound had proceeded from Mary's lips.

"Beg pardon?" said the General.

A pin might have been heard to drop, while Mary, recovering herself, said coldly,

"I think there's some mistake. I'm not Mrs. Ashforth."

"Gad, it's the old 'un!" burst in a stage whisper from Arthur Laing, who seemed determined that John Ashforth should have a wife.

The General looked to his daughter for an

explanation. Dora dared not show the emotion pictured on her face, and her back was towards the party. Charlie Ellerton was staring with a vacant look at the lady who was not Mrs. Ashforth. The worst had happened.

John came to the rescue. With an awkward laugh he said,

"Oh, you—you attribute too much happiness to me. This is Miss Travers. I—I—Her aunt, Miss Bussey, and she have kindly allowed me to join their travelling party. Miss Bussey is at that table;" and he pointed to "the old 'un."

Perhaps it was as well that at this moment the pent-up feelings which the situation and, above all, the remorseful horror with which Laing was regarding his fictitious lady's-maid, overcame Roger Deane. He burst into a laugh. After a moment the General followed heartily. Laing was the next, bettering his examples in his poignant mirth. Sir Roger sprang up.

"Come, Miss Travers," he said, "sit down. Here's the fellow who gave you your new name. Blame him," and he indicated Laing. Then he cried, "General, we must have Miss Bussey too."

The combined party, however, was not, when fully constituted by the addition of Miss Bussey, a success. Two of its members ate nothing and alternated between gloomy silence and forced gaiety; who these were may well be guessed. Mary and John found it difficult to surmount their embarrassment at the *contretemps* which had attended the introduction, or their perplexity over the cause of it. Laing was on thorns lest his distribution of parts and stations in life should be disclosed. The only bright feature was the congenial feeling which appeared at once to unite Miss Bussey and Sir Roger Deane. They sat together, and, aided by the General's geniality and Lady Deane's supramundane calm, carried the meal to a conclusion without an actual breakdown, ending up with a friendly wrangle over the responsibility for the bill. Finally, it was on Sir Roger's proposal that they all agreed to meet at five o'clock and take coffee, or what they would, together at a *café* by the water in the Bois de Boulogne. With this understanding the party broke up.

Dora and Charlie, lagging behind, found themselves alone. They hardly dared to look at one another, lest their composure should fail.

" They're not married," said Charlie.

"No."

"They've broken it off!"

"Yes."

"Because of us?"

"Yes."

"While we——"

"Yes."

"Well, in all my life, I never——"

"Oh, do be quiet."

"What an infernal ass that fellow Laing——"

"Do you think they saw anything?"

"No. I half wish they had."

"Oh, Mr. Ellerton, what shall we do? They're still in love with us!"

"Rather! They've been waiting for us."

Dora entered the hotel gates and sank into a chair in the court-yard.

"Well?" she asked helplessly; but Charlie had no suggestion to offer.

"How could they?" she broke out indignantly. "How could they break off their marriage at the last moment like that? They—they were as good as married. It's really hardly—— People should know their own minds."

She caught sight of a rueful smile on Charlie's face.

"Oh, I know; but it's different," she added impatiently. "One expects it of you; but I didn't expect it of John Ashforth."

"And of yourself?" he asked softly.

"It's all your fault, you wicked boy," she answered.

Charlie sighed heavily.

"We must break it to them," said he. "Mary will understand; she has such delicacy of feeling that——"

"You're always praising that girl. I believe you're in love with her still."

"Well, you as good as told me I wasn't fit to black Ashforth's boots."

"Anyhow he wouldn't have—have—have tried to make a girl care for him when he knew she cared for somebody else."

"Hang it, it seems to me Ashforth isn't exactly immaculate. Why, in Switzerland——"

"Never mind Switzerland, Mr. Ellerton, please."

A silence ensued. Then Charlie remarked, with a reproachful glance at Dora's averted face,

"And this is the sequel to Avignon! I shouldn't have thought a girl could change so in forty-eight hours."

Dora said nothing. She held her head very high in the air, and looked straight in front of her.

"When you gave me that kiss——" resumed Charlie.

Now this form of expression was undoubtedly ambiguous; to give a kiss may mean: 1. What it literally says—to bestow a kiss. 2. To offer one's self to be kissed. 3. To accept willingly a proffered kiss; and, without much straining of words, 4. Merely to refrain from angry expostulation and a rupture of acquaintance when one is kissed—this last partaking rather of the nature of the ratification of an unauthorised act, and being, in fact, the measure of Dora's criminality. But the other shades of meaning caught her attention.

"You know it's untrue; I never did," she cried angrily. "I told you at the time that no gentleman would have done it."

"Oh, you mean Ashforth, I suppose? It's always Ashforth."

"Well, he wouldn't."

"And some girls I know wouldn't forgive a man on Monday and round on him on Wednesday."

"Oh, you needn't trouble to mention

names.   I know the paragon you're thinking of!"

They were now at the hotel.

" Going in ? " asked Charlie.

" Yes."

" I suppose we shall go to the Bois together ? "

" I shall ask papa or Sir Roger to take me."

" Then I'll go with Lady Deane."

" I don't mind who you go with, Mr. Ellerton."

" I'll take care that you're annoyed as little as possible by my presence."

" It doesn't annoy me."

" Doesn't it, D—— ? "

" I don't notice it one way or the other."

" Oh."

" Good-bye for the present, Mr. Ellerton."

" Good-bye, Miss Bellairs; but I ought to thank you."

" What for ? "

" For making it easy to me to do what's right ; " and Charlie turned on his heel and made rapidly for the nearest *café*, where he ordered an *absinthe*.

Dora went wearily up to her bedroom, and, sitting down, reviewed the recent conversation.

She could not make out how, or why, or where they had begun to quarrel. Yet they had certainly not only begun but made very fair progress, considering the time at their disposal. It had all been Charlie's fault. He must be fond of that girl after all; if so, it was not likely that she would let him see that she minded. Let him go to Mary Travers, if—if he liked that sort of prim creature. She, Dora Bellairs, would not interfere. She would have no difficulty in finding some one who did care for her. Poor John! How happy he looked when he saw her! It was quite touching. He really looked almost—almost—— To her sudden annoyance and alarm she found herself finishing the sentence thus, " almost as Charlie did at Avignon."

" Oh, he's worth a thousand of Charlie! " she exclaimed impatiently.

At half-past four Sir Roger Deane was waiting in the hall. Presently Dora appeared.

" Where are the others ? " she asked.

" Charlie's having a drink. Your father and Maud aren't coming. They're going to rest."

" Oh, well, we might start."

"Excuse me, Miss Dora, there's some powder on your nose."

"Oh, is there? Thanks."

"What have you been powdering for?"

"Really, Sir Roger! Besides, the sun has ruined my complexion."

"Oh, the sun?"

"Yes. Don't be horrid. Do let's start."

"But Charlie——"

"I hate riding three in a cab."

"Oh, and I like riding alone in one; so——"

"No, no. You must come with me. Mr. Ellerton can follow us. He's always drinking, isn't he? I dislike it so."

Sir Roger, with a wink at an unresponsive plaster bust of *M. le Président*, followed her to the door. They had just got into their little victoria when Charlie appeared, cigarette in hand.

"Charlie," observed Deane, "Miss Bellairs thinks you'll be more comfortable by yourself than perched on this front seat."

"Especially as you're smoking," added Dora. "*Allez, cocher.*"

Charlie hailed another vehicle and got in. As he did so he remarked between his teeth, "I'm d——d if I stand it."

CHAPTER XI.

A DYNAMITE OUTRAGE.

On one side of the lake Dora and John walked together, on the other Mary and Charlie. Miss Bussey and Roger Deane sat in the garden of the *café*. The scene round them was gay. Carriages constantly drove up, discharging daintily attired ladies and their cavaliers. There was a constant stream of bicycles, some of them steered by fair riders in neat bloomer-suits; the road-waterers spread a grateful coolness in their ambit, for the afternoon was hot for the time of year, and the dust had an almost autumnal volume. Miss Bussey had been talking for nearly ten minutes on end, and now she stopped with an exhausted air, and sipped her coffee. Deane lit another cigar and sat silently looking on at the life that passed and repassed before him.

"It's a curious story," he observed at last.

" Very ; but I suppose it's all ended happily now. Look at them, Sir Roger."

" Oh, I see them."

" Their troubles are over at last, poor children ; and really I think they've all behaved very well. And yet——— "

" Yes ? "

" I should have thought Mary and Mr. Ashforth so suited to one another. Well, well, the heart's an unaccountable thing—to an old spinster, anyhow."

" You're right, Miss Bussey. Take my wife and me. You wouldn't have thought we should have hit it off, would you? First year I knew her I hardly dared to speak to her—used to mug up Browning and—(Sir Roger here referred to an eminent living writer), and chaps like that, before I went to see her, you know. No use! I bored her to death. At last I chucked it up."

" Well ? "

" And I went one day and talked about the Grand National for half an hour by the clock. Well, she asked me to come again next day, and I went, and told her all about the last burlesque and—and so on, you know. And then I asked her to marry me."

" And she said ' Yes ' ? "

"Not directly. She said there was an impassable gulf between us—an utter want of sympathy in our tastes and an irreconcilable difference of intellectual outlook."

"Dear me! Didn't that discourage you?"

"I said I didn't care a dash; she was the only girl I ever cared for (all right, Miss Bussey, don't laugh), and I'd have any outlook she liked. I said I knew I was an ass, but I thought I knew a pretty girl when I saw one, and I'd go away if she'd show me a prettier one."

"Well?"

"Well, she didn't."

Miss Bussey laughed a little.

"Of course," resumed Sir Roger, "I've got money, you know, and all that, and perhaps—— "

"Sir Roger! What a thing to say of your wife!"

"Well, with another girl—but, hang it, I don't believe Maud would. Still, you see, it's so dashed queer that sometimes—— "

"I'm sure she's very fond of you," said Miss Bussey, rather surprised at the nature of the confidence which she was receiving.

"I expect it's all right," resumed Deane,

more cheerfully; " and that brings us back to where we started, doesn't it ? "

" And we started in bewilderment."

" You're puzzled that Dora Bellairs and Ashforth should pair off together, and—— ? "

" Well, the other combination would seem more natural, wouldn't it ? Doesn't it surprise you a little ? "

" I'm never surprised at anything till I know it's true," said Sir Roger.

" What, you—— ? "

They were interrupted by the return of their friends, and a move was made. Three vehicles were necessary to take them back, for the twos could, obviously, neither be separated from one another nor united with anybody else, and in procession, Miss Bussey and Deane leading, they filed along the avenues back to the Arc de Triomphe.

They had hardly passed the open Place when their progress was suddenly arrested. A crowd spread almost across the broad road, and *sergents-de-ville* imperiously commanded a halt. There was a babble of tongues, great excitement, and a thousand eager fingers pointing at a house. The doorway was in ruins, and workmen were busy shoring it up with beams. In the middle of the crowd there was an open circle, surrounded by *gensdarmes*, and kept clear of people. In the middle of it lay a thing like a rather tall slim watering-pot, *minus* the handle. The crowd, standing on tiptoe and peeping over the shoulders of their guardians, shook their fists at this harmless-looking article and apostrophised it with a wonderful wealth of passionate invectives.

"What in the world's the matter?" cried Miss Bussey, who was nervous in a crowd.

"Revolution, I suppose," responded Deane calmly; and, turning to his nearest neighbour, he continued in the first French that came to him, "Une autre révolution, n'est-ce-pas, monsieur?"

The man stared, but a woman near him burst into a voluble explanation, from the folds of which unlearned English ears disentangled, at the third reiteration, the ominous word, "*Dynamite;*" and she pointed to the watering-pot.

"Oh, it'll go off!" shrieked Miss Bussey.

"It's gone off," said Sir Roger. "We're too late;" and there was a touch of disappointment in his voice, as he turned and shouted to the others, "Keep your seats! It's all over. Only an explosion."

"Only!" shuddered Miss Bussey. "It's a mercy we weren't killed."

It appeared that this mercy had not stopped at Miss Bussey and her friends. Nobody had been killed—not even the magistrate on the third floor for whose discipline and reformation the occurrence had been arranged; and presently the carriages were allowed to proceed.

Lady Deane's grief at having missed so interesting an occasion was very poignant.

"No, Roger," said she, "it is *not* a mere craving for horrors, or a morbid love of excitement; I wish I had been there to observe the crowd, because it's just at such moments that people reveal their true selves. The veil is lifted—the veil of hypocrisy and convention—and you see the naked soul."

"You could hear it too, Maud," observed Sir Roger. "Fine chance of improving your French vocabulary. Still, I dare say you're right."

"I'm sure I am."

Deane looked at his wife meditatively.

"You think," he asked, "that being in danger might make people——"

"Reveal their inmost natures and feelings? I'm sure of it."

" Gad !   Then we might try."

" What do you mean, Roger ? "

" Nothing.   You're going out with the General to-night ?   Very well, I shall take a turn on my own hook."

As he strolled toward the smoking-room, he met Charlie Ellerton.

" Well, old fellow, had a pleasant afternoon ? "

" Glorious ! " answered Charlie in a husky voice.

" Are we to congratulate you ? "

" I—I—well, it's not *absolutely* settled yet, Deane, but—soon, I hope."

" That's right.   Miss Bussey told me the whole story, and I think you're precious lucky to get such a girl."

" Yes, aren't I ? "

" You don't look over and above radiant."

" Do you want me to go grinning about the hotel like an infernal hyena ? "

" I think a chastened joy would be appropriate."

" Don't be an ass, Deane.   I suppose you think you're funny ? "

Sir Roger walked on, with a smile on his lips.   As he passed the reading-room Dora Bellairs came out.

"Well, Miss Dora, enjoyed your afternoon?"

"Oh, awfully—except that dreadful explosion."

"You must excuse a friend, you know. I'm awfully glad it's all come right in the end."

"You—you're very kind, Sir Roger. It's—it's—there's nothing quite settled yet."

"Oh, of course not, but still——! Well, I heard all about it, and I think he's worthy of you. I can't say more. He seems a capital fellow."

"Yes, isn't he? I——"

"Yes?"

"Oh, I'm very, very, *very* happy;" and, after making this declaration in a shaky voice, she fairly ran away down the passage. Deane watched her as she went.

"Maud's right," said he. "She always is. There's nothing for it but dynamite. I wonder where it's to be got?"

General Bellairs clapped him on the shoulders.

"Inclined for a turn, Deane? I'm going to see an old servant of mine—Painter's his name. He married my poor wife's French maid, and set up as a restaurant-keeper in the

Palais Royal. I always look him up when I come to Paris."

" I'm your man," answered Deane ; and they set out for Mr. Painter's establishment. It proved to be a neat little place, neither of the very cheap nor of the very sumptuous class, and the General was soon promising to bring the whole party to *déjeuner* there. Painter was profuse in thanks, and called madame to thank the General. The General at once entered into conversation with the trim little woman.

" Nice place yours, Painter," observed Deane.

" Pleased to hear you say so, Sir Roger."

" Very nice. Ah—er—heard of the explosion ? "

" Yes, Sir Roger. Abominable thing, sir. These Socialists——"

" Quite so. Never had one here, I suppose ? "

" No, sir. We're pretty well looked after in here."

" Like one ? " asked Deane.

" Beg pardon, sir. Ha, ha. No, sir."

" Because I want one."

" You—beg pardon, sir ? "

" Look here, Painter. I'll drop in here

after dinner for some coffee. I want to talk to you. See? Not a word to the General."

"Glad to see you, Sir Roger; but——"

"All right. I'll put you up to it. Here they come. Present me to madame."

They went away, having arranged with the Painters for luncheon and a private room on the next day but one.

"Lunch for eight," said Deane. "At least, General, I thought we might ask our friends from the European."

"Yes—and young Laing."

"Oh, I forgot him. Yes, Laing, of course. For nine—*neuf*, you know, please, madame."

"That's all right," said the General. "I'm glad to do him a turn."

"Yes, that's all right," assented Sir Roger, with the slightest possible chuckle. "We shall have a jolly lunch, eh, General?"

CHAPTER XII.

ANOTHER !

"I shall never, never forget your generosity, John."

"No, Mary. It was your honesty and courage that did it."

"I told Mr. Ellerton the whole story, and he seemed positively astonished."

"And Miss Bellairs admitted that when she wrote she considered such a thing utterly impossible. She's changed a little, Mary. She's not so cheerful and light-hearted as she used to be."

"Think what she's gone through. I've noticed just the same in Mr. Ellerton, but——"

"You hope to restore him soon?"

"Oh, well, I expect Miss Bellairs—what a pretty girl she is, John—will soon revive. too, now she is with you again. John, have you observed anything peculiar in Aunt Sarah's manner?"

"To tell you the truth, I fancied she was rather short with me once or twice at dinner."

"I believe she is—isn't pleased at—at what's happened. She hasn't taken much to Mr. Ellerton, and you know she liked you so much, that I think she still wants you as one of the family."

John laughed; then he leant forward, and said in a low voice :

"Have you settled anything about dates?"

"No. Mr. Ellerton—well, he didn't introduce the subject; so, of course, I didn't. Have you?"

"No, we haven't. I made some suggestion of the kind, but Miss Bellairs didn't fall in with it. She won't even let me ask her father's consent just yet."

"Mr. Ellerton proposes not to announce our—anything—for a few days."

"Well," said John, "I shall insist on an announcement very shortly, and you ought to do the same, Mary. We know the evils—— " He checked himself; but Mary was not embarrassed.

"Of secret engagements?" she said calmly. "We do indeed."

"Besides, it's a bore. I couldn't go with Miss Bellairs to the theatre to-night, because she said it would look too marked."

"Yes, and Mr. Ellerton said that if he dined here he might as well announce our engagement from the statue of Strasburg."

John frowned; and Mary, perceiving the bent of his thoughts, ventured to say, though with a timid air unusual to her,

"I think they're the least little bit inconsiderate, don't you, John—after all we have done for them?"

"Well, I don't mind admitting that I do feel that. I do not consider that Miss Bellairs quite appreciates the effort I have made."

Mary sighed.

"We mustn't expect too much of them, must we?" she asked.

"I suppose not," John conceded; but he still frowned.

When we consider how simple the elements of perfect happiness appear to be, regarded in the abstract, it becomes surprising to think how difficult it is to attain them in the concrete. A kind magician may grant us all we ask, may transport us whither we would go, dower us with all we lack, bring to us one desired companion after another; but something is wrong. We have a toothache, or in spite of our rich curtains there's a draught, or the loved one haps not to be at the moment congenial: and we pitifully pray the wizard to wave his wand again. Would any magician wave his for these four troublesome folk? It must be admitted that they hardly deserved it.

Nevertheless a magician was at work, and, with the expiration of the next night, his train was laid. At eleven o'clock in the forenoon of Friday Roger Deane had a final interview with the still hesitating Painter.

"But if the police should come, Sir Roger?" urged the fearful man.

"Why, you'll look a fool, that's all. Isn't the figure high enough?"

"Most liberal, Sir Roger; but—but it will alarm my wife."

"If you come to that, it'll alarm my wife."

"Very true, Sir Roger." Painter seemed to derive some comfort from this indirect community of feeling with the aristocracy.

"It'll alarm everybody, I hope. That's what it's for. Now mind—2.30 sharp—and when the coffee's been in ten minutes. Not before! I must have time for coffee."

"Very good, Sir Roger."

"Is the ladder ready?"

" Yes, Sir Roger."

" And the what's-its-name ? "

" Quite ready, Sir Roger."

" Let's see it."

It was inspected and pronounced satisfactory. Then Roger Deane set out to return to his hotel, murmuring contentedly,

" If that don't make up their minds for 'em, I don't know what will."

Then he paused suddenly.

" Gad !   Will the women have hysterics ? " he asked ; but in a moment he added, reassuring himself, " Maud never has, and, hang it, we must chance the rest."

Arrived at home he found Arthur Laing kicking his heels in the smoking-room.

" Lunching with you to-day, ain't I, somewhere in the Palais Royal ? " asked the visitor.

" Yes ; some place the General's found out. Look here, Laing, are you a nervous man ? "

" Nervous !   What do you take me for ? "

" Lose your head in moments of excitement ? "

" I never have 'em."

" Oh, well, hang you ! I say, Laing, you're not a fool. Just look here. Anything I say —*anything*, mind—at lunch to-day, you're not to contradict. You're to back me up."

" Right you are, old chap."

" And the more infernal nonsense it sounds, the more you're to take your oath about it."

" I'm there."

" And, finally, you're on no account to lay a finger either on Miss Travers or on Dora Bellairs."

" Hallo ! I'm not in the habit of beating women at any time, let alone at a lunch-party."

" I mean what I say ; you're not to touch either of them. If you do you'll spoil it. You're to go for Miss Bussey."

" She's not done me any harm."

" Never mind. As soon as the row begins, and I say, ' Save the ladies ! ' you collar Miss Bussey. See ? "

" Oh, I see. Seems to me we're going to have a lively lunch. Am I to carry the old lady ? "

" Yes."

" Oh, by Jove ! How's my biceps ? Just feel, will you ? "

Deane felt, and gravely pronounced the muscle to be equal to its task. Laing was much gratified, and awaited the unknown future with philosophic patience.

Sir Roger had predicted "a jolly lunch," but, in its early stages, the entertainment hardly earned this description. Something was wrong somewhere. Dora started by refusing, very pointedly, to sit near Charlie Ellerton; and yet, when she found herself between Ashforth and Laing, she was absent, silent, and melancholy. Charlie, on the other hand, painfully practised a laboured attentiveness to Mary Travers which contrasted ill with his usual spontaneous and gay courtesy. Miss Bussey wore an air of puzzled gravity, and Laing kept looking at her with a calculating eye. He seemed to be seeking the best grip. Lady Deane and the General, engrossed in a *tête-à-tête* discussion, did little to promote the hilarity of the table, and it was left to Deane to maintain the flow of conversation as he best could. Apparently he found the task a heavy one, for, before long, he took a newspaper out of his pocket, and, *à propos* to one of his own remarks, began to read a highly decorated account of the fearful injuries under which the last victim of the last diabolical explosion had been in danger of succumbing. Sir Roger read his gruesome narrative with much emphasis, and as he laid down the paper he observed,

"Well, I hope I'm not more of a coward than most men, but in face of dynamite—ugh!" and he shuddered realistically.

"I should make for the door," said Laing.

"Yes; but in this case the bomb was at the door!"

"Then," said Laing, "I should exit by the window."

"But this poor man," remarked Mary Travers, "stayed to rescue the woman he loved;" and her eyes rested for an instant in confident affection on Charlie Ellerton.

"We should all do as much, I trust," said John, glancing at Dora Bellairs.

"I'm sure I hope you won't have to," said Dora, rather ungraciously.

"Think what a convincing test of affection it would be," suggested Deane persuasively. "After that you could never doubt that the man loved you."

"My good Sir Roger," observed Miss Bussey, "it would be common humanity."

"Suppose there were two girls," said Laing, "and you couldn't take 'em both!"

Deane hastily interposed.

"Haven't we had enough of this dreary subject?" he asked, and he frowned slightly at Laing.

"Isn't it about time for coffee?" the General suggested.

Deane looked at his watch.

"What does the time matter, Deane, if we're ready?"

"Not a bit. 2.20. That's all right," and he rang the bell.

Painter came in with the coffee; the little man looked rather pale and nervous, but succeeded in serving the company without upsetting the cups. He came to Deane last.

"Is everything ready?" whispered that gentleman; and receiving a trembling "Yes, sir," he added, "In ten minutes."

"This," he observed out loud, "has been a pleasant gathering—a pleasant end to our outing."

"What? You're going?" asked Miss Bussey.

"Yes; my wife and I cross to England to-morrow."

"I shall go the next day," announced the General, "if Dora is ready."

John threw a glance toward Dora, but she was busy drinking her coffee.

"Well," said Deane, "I hope we may soon meet again, under equally delightful circumstances, in London. At any rate," he added, with a laugh, "there we shall be safe from——"

Crash! A loud noise came from the door, as if of some metallic substance thrown against the panels.

"Hallo!" said Laing.

"Oh, somebody tumbled downstairs," said Deane reassuringly. "Don't move, Miss Bussey."

"Oh, but, Sir Roger, what is it? What do you think? It didn't sound at all like what you say."

The General laughed.

"Come, Miss Bussey, I don't suppose it's——"

As he spoke the form of Painter appeared at the open window. He was breathless, and shrieked hastily,

"Dynamite, dynamite! Save yourselves! It'll be off in a minute."

"Then I shall be off in half a minute," said Laing.

There was a rush to the door; and Laing, remembering his instructions, joined hastily in it.

"No, no. The bomb's there!" cried Painter excitedly.

They stood still in horror for ten seconds.

"To the window, to the window, for your lives! Save the ladies!" cried Sir Roger Deane.

CHAPTER XIII.

FAITHFUL TO DEATH.

THE ladies looked at one another. Even in that awful moment, the becoming, the seemly, the dignified had its claims. The window was narrow; the ladder—Mary Travers had gone to look at it—was steep; a little, curious, excited crowd was gathering below. Deane saw their hesitation. He rushed to the door and cautiously opened it. The thing was there! Across the very entrance—that villainous oblong case! And from below came a shriek—it was madame's voice—and a cry of "Quick! quick!"

"This," said the General firmly (he had been through the Mutiny), "is not a time for punctilio. Excuse me," and he lifted Lady Deane in his stalwart arms and bore her towards the window.

With a distant reminiscence of the ball-room, Arthur Laing approached Miss Bussey, murmuring, " May I have the—— " and with a mighty effort swung the good lady from the ground. She clutched his cravat wildly, crying, " Save me ! "

Mary Travers was calmness itself. With quiet mien and unfaltering voice, she laid her hand on Charlie's arm and murmured,

" I am ready, Charlie."

At the same moment John Ashforth, the light of heroism in his eye, whispered to Dora, " You must trust yourself implicitly to me."

" Quick, quick ! " cried Deane, " or it's all up with you. Quick, Ashforth ! Quick, Charlie ; quick, man ! "

There was one more pause. Mary's hand pressed a little harder. John's arm was advancing towards Dora's waist. Sir Roger looked on with apparent impatience.

" Are you never going ? " he called. "Must I—— "

Suddenly a loud cry rang out. It came from Miss Bellairs.

" Oh, Charlie, save me, save me ! " she cried, and then and there flung herself into his arms.

" My darling ! " he whispered loudly, and catching her up made for the window. As they disappeared through it, Deane softly and swiftly opened the door and disappeared in his turn. Mary and John were left alone. Then Mary's composure gave way. Sinking into a chair, she cried,

"And I am left! Nobody cares for me. What shall I do?"

In an instant John's strong arm was round her. "I care for you!" he cried, and raising her almost senseless form, he rushed to the window. The ladder was gone!

"Gone!" he shrieked. "Where is it?"

There was no answer. The little crowd had gone too.

"We are lost," he said.

Mary opened her eyes.

"Lost!" she echoed.

"Lost! Abandoned—by those who loved —ah, no, no, Mary! In the hour of danger— then we see the truth!"

Mary's arms clasped him closer.

"Ah, John, John," she said, "we must die together, dear."

John stooped and kissed her.

Suddenly the door was opened and Deane entered. He wore a comically apologetic look, and carried an oblong metal vessel in his right hand.

"Excuse me," he said. "There's been—
er—slight but very natural mistake. It wasn't
—er—exactly dynamite — it's — er — a pre-
served-peach tin. That fool Painter——"

"Then we're safe?" cried Mary.

"Yes, thank Heaven," answered Deane
fervently.

"Oh, John!" she cried.

Sir Roger, with a smile, retired and closed
the door after him.

Downstairs Lady Deane and Miss Bussey,
forgetful of their sufferings, were restoring
Madame Painter to her senses; Painter was
uncorking a bottle of champagne for Arthur
Laing; Sir Roger Deane was talking in a low
voice and persuasive tones to an imposing
representative of the police. What passed
between them is unknown; possibly only
words, possibly something else; at any rate,
after a time, Deane smiled, the great man
smiled responsively, saluted, and disappeared,
murmuring something about *Anglais, milords,*
and *drôles.* The precise purport of his reflections could not be distinctly understood by
those in the house, for civility made him
inarticulate, but when he was safely outside
he looked at a piece of crisp paper in his
hand; then, with his thumb pointing over his

shoulder, he gave an immense shrug, and exclaimed,

"*Mais voilà un fou!*" and to this day he considers Roger Deane the very type of a maniac.

Mary and John descended. As soon as they appeared Dora jumped up from her seat and ran toward John, crying,

"Oh, Mr. Ashforth ! "

While Charlie, advancing more timidly to Mary, murmured, "Forgive me, but—— "

Mary with a slight bow, John with a lift of his hat, both without a halt or a word, passed through the room, arm-in-arm, and vanished from Mr. Painter's establishment.

Sir Roger had seized on Laing's champagne and was pouring it out. He stopped now, and looked at Dora. A sudden gleam of intelligence glanced from her eyes. Rushing up to him, she whispered, "You did it all ? It was all a hoax ? "

He nodded.

" And why ? "

" Ask Charlie Ellerton," he answered.

" Oh, but Mr. Ashforth and Mary Travers are so angry ! "

" With one another ? "

" No, with us."

Sir Roger looked her mercilessly full in the face, regardless of her blushes.

"That," he observed with emphasis; "is exactly what you wanted, Miss Bellairs."

Then he turned to the company, holding a full glass in his hand. "Ladies and gentlemen," said he, "some of us have had a narrow escape. Whether we shall be glad of it or sorry hereafter, I don't know—do you, Charlie? But here's a health to——"

But Dora, glancing apprehensively at the General, whispered, "Not yet!"

"To Dynamite!" said Sir Roger Deane.

POSTSCRIPT.

It should be added that a fuller, more graphic, and more sensational account of the outrage in the Palais Royal than this pen has been capable of inscribing will appear, together with much other curious and enlightening matter, in Lady Deane's next work. The author also takes occasion in that work—and there is little doubt that the subject was suggested by the experiences of some of her friends—to discuss the nature, quality, and duration of the Passion of Love. She concludes—if it be permissible thus far to anticipate the publication of her book—that all True Love is absolutely permanent and indestructible, untried by circumstance and untouched by time; and this opinion is, she says, endorsed by every woman who has ever been in love. Thus fortified, the conclusion seems beyond cavil. If, therefore, any incidents here recorded appear to conflict with it, we must imitate the discretion of Plato and say, either these persons were not Sons of the Gods—that is, True Lovers—or they did not do such things. Unfortunately, however, Lady Deane's proof-sheets were accessible too late to allow of the title of this story being changed. So it must stand —"The Wheel of Love;" but if any lady (men are worse than useless) will save the author's credit by proving that wheels do not go round, he will be very much obliged—and will offer her every facility.

THE LADY OF THE POOL.

CHAPTER I.

A FIRM BELIEVER.

"I SEE Mr. Vansittart Merceron's at the Court again, mamma."

"Yes, dear. Lady Merceron told me he was coming. She wanted to consult him about Charlie."

"She's always consulting him about Charlie, and it never makes any difference."

Mrs. Bushell looked up from her needle-work; her hands were full with needle and stuff, and a couple of pins protruded from her lips. She glanced at her daughter, who stood by the window in the bright blaze of a brilliant sunset, listlessly hitting the blind-cord and its tassel to and fro.

" The poor boy's very young still," mumbled Mrs. Bushell through her pins.

"He's twenty-five last month," returned Millicent. "I know, because there's exactly three years between him and me."

The sinking rays defined Miss Bushell's form with wonderful clearness. She was very tall, and the severe, well-cut cloth gown she wore set off the stately lines of her figure. She had a great quantity of fair hair and a handsome face, spoilt somewhat by a slightly excessive breadth across the cheeks; as her height demanded or excused, her hands and feet were not small, though well shaped. Would Time have arrested his march for ever, there would have been small fault to find with Nature's gifts to Miss Bushell; but, as her mother said, Millie was just what she had been at twenty-one; and Mrs. Bushell was now extremely stout. Millie escaped the inference by discrediting her mother's recollection.

The young lady wore her hat, and presently she turned away from the window, remarking,

"I think I shall go for a stroll. I've had no exercise to-day."

Either inclination, or perhaps that threatening possibility from which she strove to avert her eyes, made Millie a devotee of active pursuits. She hunted, she rode, she played lawn-tennis, and, when at the seaside, golf; when all failed, she walked resolutely four or five miles on the high road, swinging along at a healthy pace, and never pausing save to counsel an old woman or rebuke a truant urchin. On such occasions her manner (for we may not suppose that her physique aided the impression) suggested the benevolent yet stern policeman, and the vicar acknowledged in her an invaluable assistant. By a strange coincidence she seemed to suit the house she lived in—one of those large white square dwellings, devoid of ornament, yet possessing every substantial merit, and attaining, by virtue of their dimensions and simplicity, an effect of handsomeness denied to many more tricked-out buildings. The house satisfied; so did Millie, unless the judge were very critical.

"I shall just walk round by the Pool and back," she added as she opened the door.

"My dear, it's four miles!"

"Well, it's only a little after six, and we don't dine till eight."

Encountering no further opposition than a sigh of admiration—three hundred yards was the limit of pleasure in a walk to her mother—Millie Bushell started on her way, dangling a neat ebony stick in her hand, and setting her feet down with a firm, decisive tread. It did not take her long to cover the two miles between her and her destination. Leaving the road, she entered the grounds of the Court and, following a little path which ran steeply down hill, she found herself by the willows and reeds fringing the edge of the Pool. Opposite to her, on the higher bank, some seven or eight feet above the water, rose the temple, a small classical erection, used now, when at all, as a summer-house, but built to commemorate the sad fate of Agatha Merceron. The sun had just sunk, and the Pool looked chill and gloomy; the deep water under the temple was black and still. Millie's robust mind was not prone to superstition, yet she was rather relieved to think that, with the sun only just gone, there was a clear hour before Agatha Merceron would come out of the temple, slowly and fearfully descend the shallow flight of marble steps, and lay herself down in the water to die. That happened every evening, according to the legend, an hour after sunset—every evening, for the last two hundred years, since poor Agatha, bereft and betrayed, had found the Pool kinder than the world, and sunk her sorrow and her shame and her beauty there—such shame and such beauty as had never been before or after in all the generations of the Mercerons.

"What nonsense it all is!" said Millie aloud. "But I'm afraid Charlie is silly enough to believe it."

As she spoke her eye fell on a Canadian canoe, which lay at the foot of the steps. She recognised it as Charlie Merceron's, and, knowing that approach to the temple from the other side was to be gained only by a difficult path through a tangled wood, and that the canoe usually lay under a little shed a few yards from where she stood, she concluded that Charlie was in the temple. There was nothing surprising in that: it was a favourite haunt of his. She raised her voice and called to him. At first no answer came, and she repeated,

"Charlie! Charlie!"

After a moment of waiting a head was thrust out of a window in the side of the temple—a head in a straw hat.

"Hallo!" said Charlie Merceron in tones of startled surprise. Then, seeing the visitor, he added, "Oh, it's you, Millie! How did you know I was here?"

" By the canoe, of course."

" Hang the canoe ! " muttered Charlie, and his head disappeared. A second later he came out of the doorway and down the steps. Standing on the lowest, he shouted—the Pool was about sixty feet across—" What do you want ? "

" How rude you are ! " shouted Miss Bushell in reply.

Charlie got into the canoe and began to paddle across. He had just reached the other side, when Millie screamed.

" Look, look, Charlie ! " she cried. " The temple ! "

" What ? "

" I—I saw something white at the window."

Charlie got out of the canoe hastily.

" What ? " he asked again, walking up to Miss Bushell.

" I declare I saw something white at the window. Oh, Charlie ! But it's all—— "

" Bosh ? Of course it is. There's nothing in the temple."

" Well, I thought—I wonder you like to be there."

" Why shouldn't I ? "

The mysterious appearance not being repeated, Millie's courage returned.

" I thought you believed in the ghost," she said, smiling.

"So I do ; but I don't mind it."

" You've never seen it ? "

" Supposing I haven't ?   That doesn't prove it's not true."

" But you're often here at the time ? "

" Never," answered Charlie with emphasis. " I always go away before the time."

" Then you'd better come now. Put the canoe to bed and walk with me."

Charlie Merceron thrust his hands into his pockets and smiled at his companion. He was tall also, and just able to look down on her.

" No," he said, " I'm not going yet."

" How rude—oh, there it is again, Charlie ! I saw it ! I'm—I'm frightened ; " and her healthy colour paled a trifle, as she laid a hand on Charlie's arm.

" I tell you what," observed Charlie, " if you have fancies of this kind you'd better not come here any more—not in the evening, at all events. You know people who think they're going to see things always do see 'em."

" My heart is positively beating," said Miss Bushell.   " I—I don't quite like walking back alone."

"I'll see you as far as the road," Charlie conceded; and with remarkable promptitude he led the way, turning his head over his shoulder to remark,

" Really, if you're so nervous, you oughtn't to come here."

" I never will again—not alone, I mean."

Charlie had breasted the hill with such goodwill that they were already at the road.

" And you're really going back ? " she asked.

"Oh, just for a few minutes. I left my book in the temple—I was reading there. She's not due for half an hour yet, you know."

" What—what happens if you see her ? "

"Oh, you die," answered Charlie. "Good night ; " and with a smile and a nod he ran down the hill towards the Pool.

Miss Bushell, cavalierly deserted, made her way home at something more than her usual rate of speed. She had never believed in that nonsense, but there was certainly something white at that window—something white that moved. Under the circumstances, Charlie really might have seen her home, she thought, for the wood-fringed road was gloomy, and dusk coming on apace. Besides, where was the hardship in being her escort ?

Doubtless none, Charlie would have

answered, unless a man happened to have other fish to fry. The pace at which the canoe crossed the Pool and brought up at its old moorings witnessed that he had no leisure to spend on Miss Bushell. Leaping out, he ran up the steps into the temple, crying in a loud whisper,

"She's gone!"

The temple was empty, and Charlie, looking round in vexation, added,

"So has she, by Jingo!"

He sat down disconsolately on the low marble seat that ran round the little shrine. There were no signs of the book of which he had spoken to Millie Bushell. There were no signs of anybody whom he could have meant to address. Stay! One sign there was: a long hat-pin lay on the floor. Charlie picked it up with a sad smile.

"Agatha's," he said to himself.

And yet, as every one in the neighbourhood knew, poor Agatha Merceron went nightly to her phantom death bareheaded and with golden locks tossed by the wind. Moreover the pin was of modern manufacture; moreover ghosts do not wear—but there is no need to enter on debateable ground; the pin was utterly modern.

"Now, if Uncle Van," mused Charlie, "came here and saw this——!"

He carefully put the pin in his breast-pocket, and looked at his watch. It was exactly Agatha Merceron's time; yet Charlie leant back on the cold marble seat, put his hands in his pockets, and gazed up at the ceiling with the happiest possible smile on his face. For one steeped in family legends, worshipping the hapless lady's memory with warm devotion, and reputed a sincere believer in her ghostly wanderings, he awaited her coming with marvellous composure. In point of fact he had forgotten all about her, and there was nothing to prevent her coming, slipping down the steps, and noiselessly into the water, all unnoticed by him. His eyes were glued to the ceiling, the smile played on his lips, his ears were filled with sweet echoes, and his thoughts were far away. Perhaps the dead lady came and passed unseen. That Charlie did not see her was ridiculously slight evidence whereon to damn so ancient and picturesque a legend. He thought the same himself, for that night at dinner—he came in late for dinner—he maintained the credit of the story with fierce conviction against Mr. Vansittart Merceron's scepticism.

CHAPTER II.

MISS WALLACE'S FRIEND.

In old days the Mercerons had been great folk.
They had held the earldom of Langbury and
the barony of Warmley. A failure of direct
descent in the male line extinguished the
earldom; the Lady Agatha was the daughter
of the last earl, and would have been Baroness
Warmley had she lived. On her death that
title passed to her cousin, and continued in
that branch till the early days of the present
century. Then came another break. The
Lord Warmley of that day, a Regency dandy,
had a son, but not one who could inherit his
honours, and away went the barony to a yet
younger branch, where, falling a few years
later into female hands, it was merged in a
brand new viscounty, and was now waiting
till chance again should restore it to an independent existence. From the Mercerons
of the Court it was gone for ever, and the

blot on their escutcheon which lost it them
was a sore point, from which it behoved
visitors and friends to refrain their tongues.
The Regent had, indeed, with his well-known
good nature, offered a baronetcy to hide the
stain ; but pride forbade, and the Mercerons
now held no titles, save the modest dignity
which Charlie's father, made a K.C.B. for
services in the North-West Provinces, had
left behind him to his widow. But the old
house was theirs, and a comfortable remnant
of the lands, and the pictures of the extinct
earls and barons, down to him whose sins
had robbed the line of its surviving rank and
left it in a position, from an heraldic point
of view, of doubtful respectability. Lady
Merceron felt so acutely on the subject that
she banished this last nobleman to the
smoking-room. There was, considering
everything, an appropriateness in that
position, and he no longer vexed her eyes as
she sat at meat in the dining-room. She had
purposed a like banishment for Lady Agatha ;
but here Charlie had intereded, and the
unhappy beauty hung still behind his mother's
chair and opposite his own. It was just to
remember that but for poor Agatha's fault
and fate the present branch might never have

enjoyed the honours at all; so Charlie urged to Lady Merceron, catching at any excuse for keeping Lady Agatha. Lady Merceron's way of judging pictures may seem peculiar, but the fact is that she lacked what is called the sense of historical perspective : she did not see why our ancestors should be treated so tenderly and allowed, with a charitable reference to the change in manners, forgiveness for what none to-day could hope to win pardon for. Mr. Vansittart Merceron smiled at his sister-in-law and shrugged his shoulders ; but in vain. To the smoking-room went the wicked Lord Warmley, and Lady Agatha was remarkably lucky in that she did not follow him.

Mr. Vansittart, half-brother to the late Sir Victor, and twenty years younger than he, was a short thick-set man, with a smooth round white face, and a way of speaking so deliberate and weighty that it imparted momentousness to nothings and infallibility to nonsense. When he really had something sensible to say, and that was very fairly often, the effect was enormous. He was now forty-six, a widower, well off by his marriage, and a Member of Parliament. Naturally Lady Merceron relied much on his advice, especially in what concerned her son; she was hazy about the characters and needs of young men, not knowing how they should be treated or what appealed to them. Amid her haziness, one fact only stood out clear. To deal with a young man, you wanted a man of the world. In this capacity Mr. Vansittart had now been sent for to the Court, the object of his visit being nothing less than the arrangement and satisfactory settlement of Charlie's future.

Mr. Vansittart approached the future through the present and the past.

"You wasted your time at school, you wasted your time at Oxford, you're wasting your time now," he remarked, when Charlie and he were left alone after dinner.

Charlie was looking at Lady Agatha's picture. With a sigh he turned to his uncle.

"That's all very well," he said tolerantly; "but what is there for me to do?"

"If you took more interest in country pursuits it might be different. But you don't hunt, you shoot very seldom——"

"And very badly."

"And not at all well, as you admit. You say you won't become a magistrate, you show no interest in politics or—er—social questions. You simply moon about."

" Oh, I know what's being arranged for you."

" So do I."

" And you'll do it. Oh, you think you won't; but you will. Men always end by doing what they're told."

" Does Mr. Marland ? "

" He begins by it," laughed his wife.

" Is that why he's not coming till Saturday week ? "

" Mr. Merceron ! But what was Miss Bushell doing at the Pool ? Did she come to find you ? "

" Oh, no ; just for a walk."

" Poor girl ! "

" Why ? It's good for her."

" I didn't mean the walk."

" I'd blush if there was light enough to make it any use, Mrs. Marland."

" Oh, but I know there's something. You don't go there every evening to look for a dead lady, Mr. Merceron."

Charlie stopped short, and took his cigar from his mouth.

" What ? " he asked, a little abruptly.

" Well, I shall follow you some day, and I shouldn't be surprised if I met—not Agatha —but—— "

" Well ? " asked Charlie, with an uncertain smile.

" Why, poor Miss Bushell ! "

Charlie laughed and replaced his cigar.

" What are we standing still for ? " he said.

" I don't know. You stopped. She'd be such an ideal match for you."

" Then I should never have done for you, Mrs. Marland."

" My dear boy, I was married when you were still in Eton collars."

They had completed the circuit of the garden, and now approached where Lady Merceron sat, enveloped in a shawl.

" Charlie ! " she called. " Here's a letter from Victor Sutton. He's coming to-morrow."

" I didn't know you'd asked him," said Charlie, with no sign of pleasure at the news. Victor had been at school and college with Charlie, and often, in his holidays, at the Court, for he was Sir Victor's godson. Yet Charlie did not love him. For the rest, he was very rich, and was understood to cut something of a figure in London society.

" Mr. Sutton? Oh, I know him," exclaimed Mrs. Marland. " He's charming ! "

" Then ! you shall entertain him," said Charlie. " I resign him."

" I can't think why you're not more pleased to have him here, Charlie," remarked Lady Merceron. "He's very popular in London, isn't he, Vansittart?"

"I've met him at some very good houses," answered Mr. Vansittart. And that, he seemed to imply, is better than mere popularity.

"The Bushells were delighted with him last time he was here," continued Lady Merceron.

"There! A rival for you!" Mrs. Marland whispered.

Charlie laughed cheerfully. Sutton would be no rival of his, he thought; and if he and Millie liked one another, by all means let them take one another. A month before he would hardly have dismissed the question in so summary a fashion, for the habit of regarding Millie as a possibility, and her readiness as a fact, had grown strong by the custom of years, and, far as he was from a passion, he might not have enjoyed seeing her allegiance transferred to Victor Sutton. Certainly he would have suffered defeat from that hand with very bad grace. Now, however, everything was changed.

· "Vansittart," said Lady Merceron, "Charlie and I want to consult you" (she often coupled

Charlie's hypothetical desire for advice with her own actual one in appeals to Mr. Vansittart) "about Mr. Prime's rent."

"Oh, at the old farm?"

"Yes. He wants another reduction."

"He'll want to be paid for staying there next."

"Well, poor man, he's had to take lodgers this summer—a thing he's never done before. Charlie, did you know that?"

"Yes," said Charlie, interrupting an animated conversation which he had started with Mrs. Marland.

"Do you know who they are?" pursued his mother, wandering from Mr. Prime's rent to the more interesting subject of his lodgers.

"Ladies from London," answered Charlie.

"Rather vague," commented Mr. Vansittart. "Young ladies or old ladies, Charlie?"

"Why does he want to know?" asked Mrs. Marland; but chaff had about as much effect on Mr. Vansittart as it would have on an ironclad. He seemed not to hear, and awaited an answer with a bland smile. In truth, he thought Mrs. Marland a silly woman.

"Young, I believe," answered Charlie in a careless tone.

"It's curious I've not seen them about,"

said Lady Merceron. "I pass the farm almost every day. Who are they, Charlie?"

"One's a Miss Wallace. She's engaged to Willie Prime."

"To Willie? Fancy!"

"H'm! I think," remarked Mr. Vansittart, "that, from the point of view of a reduction of rent, these lodgers are a delusion. Of course she stays with Prime if she's going to marry his son."

"Fancy Willie!" reiterated Lady Merceron. "Surely he can't afford to marry? He's in a bank, you know, Vansittart, and he only gets a hundred and twenty pounds a-year."

"One blessing of the country is that everybody knows his neighbour's income," observed Mr. Vansittart.

"Perhaps the lady has money," suggested Mrs. Marland. "But, Mr. Merceron, who's the other lady?"

"A friend of Miss Wallace's, I believe. I don't know her name."

"Oh, they're merely friends of Prime's?" Mr. Vansittart concluded. "If that's all he bases his claim for a reduction on——"

"Hang it! He might as well have it," interrupted Charlie. "He talks to me about it for half an hour every time we meet."

"But, my dear Charlie, you have more time than money to waste—at least, so it seems."

His uncle's sarcasm never affected Charlie's temper.

"I'll turn him on to you, uncle," he replied, " and you can see how you like it."

"I'll go and call on him to-morrow. You'd better come too, Charlie."

"And then you can see the ladies from London," added Mrs. Marland. " Perhaps the one who isn't young Mr. Prime's will be interesting."

"Or," said Charlie, " as mostly happens in this woeful world, the one who is."

"I think the less we see of that sort of person at all, the better," observed Lady Merceron with gentle decision. " They can hardly be *quite* what we're accustomed to."

"That sort of person ! "

Charlie went to bed with the phrase ringing in his horror-struck ears. If to be the most beautiful, the most charming, and the most refined, the daintiest, the wittiest and prettiest, the kindest and the sweetest, the merriest and most provoking creature in the whole world—if to be all this were yet not to weigh against being " that sort of person "

—if it were not, indeed, to outweigh, banish, and obliterate everything else—why, the world was not fit to live in, and he no true Merceron! For the Merceron men had always pleased themselves.

CHAPTER III.

ALL NONSENSE.

On the evening of the next day, while the sun was still on the Pool, and its waters, forgetful of darker moods and bygone tragedies, smiled under the tickling of darting golden gleams, a girl sat on the broad lowest step of the temple. She had rolled the sleeves of her white gown above her elbow, up well-nigh to her shoulder, and, the afternoon being sultry, from time to time dipped her arms in the water and, taking them out again, amused herself by watching the bright drops race down to her rosy finger-tips. The sport was good, apparently, for she laughed and flung back her head so that the stray locks of hair might not spoil her sight of it. On either side of this lowest step there was a margin of smooth level grass, and, being unable as she sat to bathe both arms at once, presently she moved on to the grass and lay down, sinking her elbows in the pond and leaning her face over the edge of it. The posture had another advantage she had not thought of, and she laughed again when she saw her own eyes twinkling at her from the depths. As she lay there a longing came upon her.

" If I could be sure he wouldn't come I'd dip my feet," she murmured.

As, however, he had come every evening for a fortnight past the fancy was not to be indulged, and she consoled herself by a deeper dive yet of her arms, and by drooping her head till her nose and the extreme fringe of her eyelashes were wetted, while the stray locks floated on either side.

Presently, as she still looked, she saw another shadow on the water, and exchanged with her image a confidential glance.

" You again ? " she asked.

The other shadow nodded.

" Why didn't you come in the canoe ? "

" Because people see it."

It struck her that her attitude was unconventional, and by a lithe complicated movement, whereof Charlie noticed only the elegance and not the details, she swept round, and, sitting, looked up at him.

" I know who she was," she observed.

" She very nearly knew who you were. You oughtn't to have come to the window."

" She thought I was the ghost."

" You shouldn't reckon on people being foolish."

" Shouldn't I? Yet I reckoned on your coming—or there'd have been some more of me in the water."

" I wish I were an irregular man," said Charlie.

She was slowly turning down her sleeves, and, ignoring his remark, said, with a question in her tones,

" Nettie Wallace says that Willie Prime says that everybody says that you're going to marry that girl."

" I believe it's quite true."

" Oh ! " and she looked across the Pool.

" True that everybody says so," added Charlie. " Why do you turn down your sleeves ? "

" How funny I must have looked, sprawling on the bank like that ! " she remarked.

" Awful ! " said Charlie, sitting down.

She looked at him with uneasiness in her eye.

" Nothing but an ankle, I swear," he answered.

She blushed and smiled.

" I think you should whistle, or something, as you come."

" Not I," said Charlie with decision.

Suddenly she turned to him with a serious face, or one that tried to be serious.

" Why do you come ? " she asked.

" Why do I eat ? " he returned.

" And yet you were angry the first time."

" Nobody likes to be caught ranting out poetry—especially his own."

" I believe you were frightened—you thought I was Agatha. The poetry was about her, wasn't it ? "

" It's not at all a bad poem," observed Charlie.

" You remember I liked it so much that I clapped my hands."

" And I jumped ! "

The girl laughed.

" Ah, well," she said, " it's time to go home."

" Oh dear no," said Charlie.

" But I've promised to be early, because Willie Prime's coming, and I'm to be introduced to him."

" Willie Prime can wait. He's got Miss Wallace to comfort him, and I've got nobody to comfort me."

"Oh yes.   Miss Bushell."

"You know her name?"

"Yes—and yours—your surname, I mean; you told me the other."

"That's more than you've done for me."

"I told you my name was Agatha."

"Ah, but that was a joke.   I'd been talking about Agatha Merceron."

"Very well.   I'm sorry it doesn't satisfy you.   If you won't believe me——!"

"But your surname?"

"Oh, mine?   Why, mine's Brown."

"Brown!" re-echoed Charlie, with a tinge of disappointment in his tone.

"Don't you like it?" asked Miss Agatha Brown, with a smile.

"Oh, it will do for the present," laughed Charlie.

"Well, I don't mean to keep it all my life.   I've spent to-day, Mr. Merceron, in spying out your house.   Nettie Wallace and I ventured quite near.   It's very pretty."

"Rather dilapidated, I'm afraid."

"What's the time, Mr. Merceron?"

"Half-past six.   Oh, by Jove!"

"Well?   Afraid of seeing poor Agatha?"

"I should see nobody but you, if you were here.   No.   I forgot that I've got to meet

some one at the station at a quarter-past seven."

"Oh, do tell me who!"

"You'd be none the wiser. It's a Mr. Victor Sutton."

"Victor Sutton!" she exclaimed, with a glance at Charlie which passed unnoticed by him. "Is he a friend of yours?"

"I suppose so. Of my family's, anyhow."

"Good-bye. I'm going," she announced.

"You'll be here to-morrow?"

"Yes. For the last time."

She dropped this astounding thunderbolt on Charlie's head as though it had been the most ordinary remark in the world.

"The last time! Oh, Miss——" No; somehow he could not lay his tongue to that "Miss Brown."

"I can't spend all my life in Laug Marsh," said she.

"Agatha!" he burst out.

"No, no. This is not the last time. Shan't we keep that?" she asked, with a provokingly light-hearted smile.

"You promise to be here to-morrow?"

"Oh yes."

"I shall have something to say to you then," Charlie announced with a significant air.

" Oh, you never lack conversation."

" You'll be here at five ? "

" Precisely," she answered with mock gravity ; " and now I'm gone ! "

Charlie took off his straw hat, stretched out his right hand, and took hers. For a moment she drew back ; but he looked very handsome and gallant as he bowed his head down to her hand, and she checked the movement.

" Oh, well ! " she murmured ; she was protesting against any importance being attached to the incident.

Charlie, having paid his homage, walked, or rather ran, swiftly away. To begin with, he had none too much time if he was to meet Victor Sutton ; secondly, he was full of a big resolve, and that generally makes a man walk fast.

The lady pursued a more leisurely progress. Swinging her hat in her hand, she made her way through the tangled wood back to the high road, and turned towards Mr. Prime's farm. She went slowly along, thinking, perhaps, of the attractive young fellow she had left behind her, wondering, perhaps, why she had promised to meet him again. She did not know why, for there was sure to happen at that last meeting the one thing which she did not, she supposed, wish to happen. However a promise is a promise. She heard the sound of wheels behind her, and, turning, found the farmer's spring-cart hard on her heels. The farmer was driving, and by his side sat a nice-looking girl dressed in the extreme of fashion. On the back seat was a young man in a very light suit, with a fine check pattern, and a new pair of brown leather shoes. The cart pulled up.

" We can make room for ye, miss," said old Mr. Prime.

Nettie Wallace jumped up and stood with her foot on the step. Willie Prime jumped down and effected her transfer to the back seat. Agatha climbed up beside the farmer and stretched her hand back to greet Willie. Willie took it rather timidly. He did not quite " savvy " (as he expressed it to himself); his *fiancée's* friend was very simply attired, infinitely more simply than Nettie herself. Nettie had told him that her friend was " off and on " (a vague and rather obscure qualification of the statement) in the same line as herself—namely, Court and high-class dressmaking. Yet there was a difference between Nettie and her friend.

"Anybody else arrived by the train?" asked Agatha.

"A visitor for the Court. A good-looking gentleman, wasn't he, Willie?"

Nettie was an elegant creature, and, but for the "gentleman," and that slight but ineradicable twang that clings like Nessus' shirt to the cockney, all effort and all education notwithstanding (it will even last three generations, and is audible, perhaps, now and then in the House of Lords), her speech was correct, and even dainty in its prim nicety.

"Ah!" said Agatha.

"His name's Sutton," said Willie; "Mr. Charles—young Mr. Merceron—told me so when he was talking to me on the platform."

"You know young Mr. Merceron?" asked Agatha.

"Why, they was boys together," interrupted the old farmer, who made little of the refinements of speech. In his youth no one, from the lord to the labourer, spoke grammar in the country. "Used to larn to swim together in the Pool, didn't you, Willie?"

"I must have a dip there to-morrow," cried Willie; and Agatha wondered what time he would choose. "And I'll take you there, Nettie. Ever been yet?"

" No.   They—they say it's haunted, don't they, Willie ? "

" That's nonsense," said Willie.   London makes a man sceptical.   The old farmer shook his head and grunted doubtfully.   His mother had seen poor Agatha Merceron ; this was before the farmer was born—a little while before—and the shock had come nigh to being most serious to him.   The whole countryside knew it.

" Why do you call it nonsense, Mr. Prime ? " asked Agatha.

" Oh, I don't know, Miss——"

" Miss Brown, Willie," said Nettie.

" Miss Brown.   Anyway, we needn't go the time the ghost comes."

" I should certainly avoid that," laughed Agatha.

" We'll go in the morning, Nettie, and I'll have my swim in the evening.

Agatha frowned.   It would be particularly inconvenient if Willie Prime took his swim in the evening."

" Oh, don't, Willie," cried Nettie.   " She —she might do you some harm."

Willie was hard to persuade.   He was not above liking to appear a daredevil ; and the discussion was still raging when they reached

the farm.   The two girls went upstairs to the
little rooms which they occupied.   Agatha
turned into hers, and Nettie Wallace followed
her.

" Your Willie is very nice," said Agatha,
sitting on her bed.

Nettie smiled with pleasure.

" And, now that you've other company, I
shall go."

" You're going, miss ? "

" Not *miss*."

Nettie laughed.

" I forget sometimes," she said.

" Well, you must remember just over to-
morrow.   I shall go next day.   I must meet
my grandfather in London."

Nettie offered no opposition.   On the contrary, she appeared rather relieved.

" Nettie, did you like Mr. Sutton's looks ? "
asked Agatha, after a pause.

" He's too black and blue for my taste,"
answered Nettie.

Willie Prime was red and yellow.

" Blue ?   Oh, you mean his cheeks ? "

" Yes.   But he's a handsome gentleman all
the same ; and you should have seen his
luggage ! Such a dressing-bag—cost fifty
pounds, I dare say."

"Oh dear me!" said Agatha. "Yes, Nettie, I shall go the day after to-morrow."

"Mr. Merceron asked to be introduced to me," said Nettie proudly. "And he asked where you were—he said he'd seen you at the window."

"Did he?" said Agatha negligently; and Nettie, finding the conversation flag, retired to her own room.

Agatha sat a moment longer on the bed.

"What a very deceitful young man," she exclaimed at last. "I must be a very strict secret indeed. Well, I suppose I should be."

CHAPTER IV.

A CATASTROPHE AT THE POOL.

MR. VANSITTART MERCERON was not quite sure that Victor Sutton had any business to call him "Merceron." He was nearly twenty years older than Victor, and a man of considerable position; nor was he, as some middle-aged men are, flattered by the implication of contemporaneousness carried by the mode of address. But it is hard to give a hint to a man who has no inkling that there is room for one; and when Mr. Vansittart addressed Victor as "Mr. Sutton," the latter graciously told him to "hang the Mister." Reciprocity was inevitable, and the elder man asked himself, with a sardonic grin, how soon he would be "Van."

"Coming to bathe, Merceron?" he heard under his window at eight o'clock the next morning. "We're off to the Pool."

Mr. Vansittart shouted an emphatic negative, and the two young fellows started off by themselves. Charlie's manner was affected by the ceremonious courtesy which a well-bred host betrays towards a guest not very well beloved; but Victor did not notice this. It seldom occurred to him that people did not like him.

"Yes," he was saying, "I'm just twenty-nine. I've had my fling, Charlie, and now I shall get to business."

Charlie was relieved to find that according to this reckoning he had several more years' "fling" before him.

"Next year," pursued Victor, "I shall marry; then I shall go into Parliament, and then I shall go ahead."

"I didn't know you were engaged."

"No, I'm not, but I'm going to be. I can please myself, you see; I've got lots of coin."

"Oh, yes, but can you please the lady?" asked Charlie.

"My dear boy," began Victor, "when you've seen a little more of the world——"

"Here we are," said Charlie. "Why, hallo! Who's that?"

A dripping head and a blowing mouth were visible in the middle of the Pool.

"Willie Prime, by Jove! 'Morning,

Willie;" and Charlie set about flinging off his flannels, Victor following his example in a more leisurely fashion.

Willie Prime was a little puzzled to know how he ought to treat Charlie. "Charlie" he had been in very old days—then Master Charlie (that was Willie's mother's doing)—then Mr. Charles. But now Willie had set up for himself. He had played billiards with a lord, and football against the Sybarites, and, incidentally, hobnobbed with quite great people. It is not very easy to assert a social position when one has nothing on, and only one's head out of water, but Willie did it.

"Good morning—er—Merceron," said he.

Victor heard him, and put up his eyeglass in amazement; but he, in his turn, had only a shirt on, and the *hauteur* was a failure. Charlie utterly failed to notice the incident.

"Is it cold?" he shouted.

"Beastly," answered Willie. The man who has got in always tells the man who is going to get in that it is "beastly cold."

"Here goes!" cried Charlie; and a minute later he was treading water by Willie's side.

"Miss Wallace all fit?" he asked.

"Thank you, yes, she's all right."

"And her friend?"

" All right, I believe."

" And when is it to be, old fellow ? "

" Soon as I get a rise."

" What ? " asked the unsophisticated Charlie, who knew the phrase chiefly in connection with fish.

" A rise of screw, you know."

" Oh, ah, yes—what a fool I am ! " and Charlie disappeared beneath the waves.

When they were all on the bank, drying, Willie, encouraged by not being discouraged (save by Sutton's silence) in his advances, ventured further, and asked in a joking tone,

" And aren't you marked off yet ? We've been expecting to hear of it for the last twelve months."

" What do you mean ? "

" Why, you and Miss Bushell."

Charlie struggled through his shirt, and then answered, with his first touch of distance,

" Nothing in it. People've got no business to gossip."

" It's damned impertinent," observed Victor Sutton in slow and deliberate tones.

Willie flushed.

" I beg pardon," he said gruffly. " I only repeated what I heard."

"My dear fellow, no harm's done," cried Charlie. "Who was the fool?"

"Well—in fact—my father."

The situation was awkward, but they wisely eluded it by laughter. But a thought struck Charlie.

"I say, did your father state it as a fact?"

"Oh no; but as a certainty, you know."

"When?"

"Last night at supper."

Charlie's brow clouded. Miss B——, that is, Agatha, was certain to have been at supper. However all that could be put right in the evening — that one blessed evening left to him. He looked at Willie and opened his mouth to speak; but he shut it again. It did not seem to him that he could question Willie Prime about the lady. She had chosen to tell him nothing, and her will was his law. But he was yearning to know what she was and how she came there. He refrained; and this time virtue really had a reward beyond itself, for Willie would blithely have told him that she was a dressmaker (he called Nettie, however, the manager of a Court *modiste's* business), and that would not have pleased Charlie.

It was all very well for Charlie to count on

that blessed evening; but he reckoned without his host—or rather without his guests.

The Bushells came to lunch, Millie driving her terrified mother in a lofty gig; and at lunch Millie recounted her vision of Agatha Merceron. She did not believe it, of course; but it was queer, wasn't it? Victor Sutton rose to the bait at once.

"We'll investigate it," he cried. "Merceron" (he meant the patient Mr. Vansittart), "didn't you once write an article on 'Apparitions' for *Intellect*"?

"Yes, I proved there were none," answered Mr. Vansittart.

"That's impossible, you know," remarked Mrs. Marland gently.

"We'll put you to the proof this very evening," declared Mr. Sutton.

Charlie started.

"Are you game, Miss Bushell?" continued Victor.

"Ye—yes, if you'll keep quite near me," answered Millie, with a playful shudder. Charlie reflected how ill playfulness became her, and frowned. But Millie was pleased to see him frown; she enjoyed showing him that other men liked to keep quite near to her.

"Then this evening we'll go in a body to the Pool."

"I shall not go," shuddered Mrs. Marland.

"An hour after sunset!"

"Half an hour. She might be early—and we'll stay half an hour after. We'll give her a fair show."

"Come," thought Charlie, "I shall get an hour with Agatha."

"You'll come, Charlie?" asked Victor.

"Oh, all right," he answered, hiding all signs of vexation. He could get back by six and join the party. But why was Mrs. Marland looking at him?

The first step, however, towards getting back is to get there, and Charlie found this none so easy. After lunch came lawn-tennis, and he was impressed. Mr. Vansittart played a middle-aged game, and Victor had found little leisure for this modest sport among his more ambitious amusements. Charlie had to balance Millie Bushell, and he spent a very hot and wearying afternoon. They would go on ; Victor declared it was good for him, Uncle Van delighted in a hard game (it appeared to be a very hard game to him from the number of strokes he missed), and Millie grew in vigour, ubiquity, and (it must be added) intensity of colour as the hours wore away. It was close on five before Charlie, with a groan, could throw down his racquet.

"Poor boy!" said Mrs. Marland.

"Charlie dear," called Lady Merceron, who had been talking comfortably to Mrs. Bushell in the shade, "come and hand the tea. I'm sure you must all want some. Millie, my dear, how hot you look!"

"She never will take any care of her complexion," complained Mrs. Bushell.

"Take care of your stom—your health—and your complexion will take care of itself," observed Mr. Vansittart.

"Charlie! Where is the boy?" called Lady Merceron again.

The boy was gone. He was flying as fast as his legs would take him to the Pool. Where was that cherished interview now? He could hope only for a few wretched minutes—hardly enough to say good-bye once —before he must hustle —yes, positively hustle—Agatha out of sight. He had heard that abominable Sutton remark that they might as well start directly after tea.

He was breathless when he burst through the willows. But there he came to a sudden, a dead stop, and then drew back into shelter again. There on the bank, scarcely a dozen feet from it, sat two people—a young man with his arm round a young woman's waist. Willie Prime and Nettie Wallace, "by all that's damnable!" as Sir Peter says! Charlie said something quite as forcible.

He felt for his watch, but he had left it with his waistcoat on the lawn. What was the time? Was it going quickly or slowly? Could he afford to wait, or must he run round to the road and intercept Agatha? Five minutes passed in vacillation.

"I'll go and stop her," he said, and began a cautious retreat. As he moved he heard Willie's voice.

"Well, my dear, let's be off," said Willie.

Nettie rose with a sigh of content, adjusted her hat coquettishly, and smoothed her skirts.

"I'm ready, Willie. It's been beautiful, hasn't it?"

They came towards Charlie. Evidently they intended to regain the road by the same path as he had chosen. Indeed, from that side of the Pool there was no choice, unless one clambered round by the muddy bank.

"We must make haste," said Willie. "Father'll want his tea."

If they made haste they would be close on

his heels. Charlie shrank back behind a willow and let them go by; then, quick as thought, rushed to his canoe and paddled across; up the steps and into the temple he rushed. She wasn't there! Fate is too hard for the best of us sometimes. Charlie sat down and, stretching out his legs, stared gloomily at his toes.

Thus he must have sat nearly ten minutes, when a head was put round the Corinthian pilaster of the doorway.

" Poor boy ! Am I very late ? "

Charlie leapt up and forward, breathlessly blurting out joy tempered by uneasiness. Agatha gathered the difficulty of the position.

" Well," said she, smiling, " I must disappear, and you must go back to your friends."

" No," said Charlie; " I must talk to you."

" But they may come any moment."

" I don't care ! "

" Oh, but I do. Charlie—— What's the matter? Oh, didn't I ever call you ' Charlie ' before? Well, Charlie, if you love me (yes, I know !) you'll not let these people see me."

" All right ! Come along. I'll take you to the road and come back. Hallo ! What's that ? "

"It's them!" exclaimed the lady.

It was. The pair dived back into the temple. On the opposite bank stood Millie Bushell, Mr. Vansittart, and Victor Sutton.

"Hallo, there, Charlie, you thief!" cried Victor. "Bring that canoe over here. Miss Bushell wants to get to the temple."

"Hush! Don't move!" whispered Agatha.

"But they know I'm here; they see that confounded canoe."

"Charlie! Charlie!" was shouted across in three voices.

"What the devil——" muttered Charlie.

"They mustn't see me," urged Agatha.

Victor Sutton's voice rose clear and distinct.

"I'll unearth him!" he cried. "I know the way round. You wait here with Miss Bushell, Merceron."

"Oh, he's coming round!"

"I must chance it," said Charlie, and he came out of hiding. A cry greeted him. Victor was already started, but stopped. Charlie embarked and shot across.

"You villain! You gave us the slip," cried Uncle Van.

Miss Bushell began quietly to embark. Uncle Van followed her example.

" Oh, Mr. Merceron, you'll sink us ! " cried Millie.

Charlie sat glum and silent. The situation beat him completely.

Uncle Van drew back. Millie seized the paddle and propelled the canoe out from the bank.

" You come round with me, Merceron," called Sutton, and the two men turned to the path. " No," added Victor. " Look here, we can climb round here ; " and he pointed to the bank. There was a little narrow muddy track ; but it was enough.

The canoe was halfway across ; the two men—Victor leading at a good pace—were halfway round. Charlie glanced at the window of the temple and caught a fleeting glance of a despairing face. " If you love me, they mustn't see me ! "

" Here, give me the paddle ! " he exclaimed, and reached forward for it.

" No, I can do it," answered Millie, lifting the instrument out of his reach.

Charlie stepped forward—rather, he jumped forward, as a man jumps over a ditch. There was a shriek from Millie ; the canoe swayed, tottered, and upset. In a confused mass, Millie Bushell and Charlie were hurled into the water. Victor and Uncle Van, hardly five yards from the steps, turned in amazement.

"Help! help!" screamed Millie.

"Help!" echoed Charlie. "I can't hold her up. Victor, come and help me! Uncle Van, come along!"

"The devil!" murmured Uncle Van.

"Quick, quick!" called Charlie; and Victor, with a vexed laugh, peeled off his coat and jumped in. Mr. Vansittart stood with a puzzled air. Then a happy thought struck him. He turned and trotted back the way he had come. He would get a rope!

As he went, as Victor reached the strugglers in the water, a slim figure in white, with a smile on her face, stole cautiously from the temple and disappeared in the wood behind. Charlie saw her go, but he held poor Millie's head remorselessly tight towards the other bank.

And that was the last he saw of the Lady of the Pool.

Millie Bushell landed, her dripping clothes clinging round her. Victor was shivering, for the evening had turned chilly. Uncle Van had a bit of rope from the boat-shed in his hand, and a doubtful smile on his face.

"We'd best get Miss Bushell home," he suggested ; and they started in gloomy procession. Charlie, in remorse, gave Millie his arm.

"Oh, how could you?" she murmured piteously. She was cold, she was wet, and she was sure that she looked frightful.

"I—I didn't do it on purpose," Charlie blurted out eagerly.

"On purpose ! Well, I suppose not," she exclaimed, bewildered.

Charlie flushed. Victor shot a swift glance at him.

Halfway home they met Mrs. Marland, and the whole affair had to be explained to her. Charlie essayed the task.

"Still, I don't see how you managed to upset the canoe," observed Mrs. Marland.

"No more do I," said Victor Sutton.

Charlie gave it up.

"I'm so sorry, Millie," he whispered. "You must try to forgive me."

So, once again, the coast was left clear for Agatha Merceron, if she came that night. But, whether she did or not, the other Agatha came no more, and Charlie's great resolve went unfulfilled. Yet the next evening he went alone to the temple, and he found, lying on the floor, a little handkerchief trimmed with lace and embroidered with the name of "Agatha." This he put in his pocket, thanking Heaven that his desperate manœuvre had kept the shrine inviolate the day before.

"Poor Millie!" said he. "But then I had to do it."

"I hear," remarked Lady Merceron a few days later, "that one of Mr. Prime's friends has left him—not Willie's young lady—the other."

"Has she?" asked Charlie.

No one pursued the subject, and, after a moment's pause, Mrs. Marland, who was sitting next Charlie, asked him in a low voice whether he had been to the Pool that evening.

"No," answered Charlie. "I don't go every night."

"Oh, poor dear Miss Bushell!" laughed Mrs. Marland; and, when Charlie looked inquiringly at her, she shook her head.

"You see, I know something of young men," she explained.

CHAPTER V.

AN UNFORESEEN CASE.

" I wish to goodness," remarked the Reverend Sigismund Taylor, rubbing the bridge of his nose with a corner of the Manual, " that the Vicar had never introduced Auricular Confession. It may be in accordance with the practice of the Primitive Church, but—one does meet with such very curious cases. There's nothing the least like it in the Manual."

He opened the book and searched its pages over again. No, the case had not been foreseen. It must be included in those which were " left to the discretion of the priest."

" It's a poor Manual," said Mr. Taylor, throwing it down and putting his hands in the pocket of his cassock. " Poor girl! She was quite distressed, too. I must have something to tell her when she comes next week."

Mr. Taylor had, in face of the difficulty,

taken time to consider, and the penitent had gone away in suspense. To represent one's self as a dressmaker—well, there was nothing very outrageous in that; it was unbecoming, but venial, to tell sundry fibs by way of supporting the assumed character—the Manual was equal to that; but the rest of the disclosure was the *crux.* Wrong, no doubt, was the conduct—but how wrong? That made all the difference. And then there followed another question: What ought to be done? She had asked for advice about that also, and, although such counsel was not strictly incumbent on him, he felt that he ought not to refuse it. Altogether he was puzzled. At eight and twenty one cannot be ready for everything; yet she had implored him to consult nobody else, and decide for her himself. "I've such trust in you," she had said, wiping away an incipient teardrop; and, although Mr. Taylor told her that the individual was nothing and the Office everything, he had been rather gratified. Thinking that a turn in the open air might clear his brain and enable him better to grapple with this very thorny question, he changed his cassock for a long-tailed coat, put on his wideawake, and, leaving the precincts of St.

Edward Confessor, struck across Park Lane and along the Row. He passed several people he knew, both men and women : Mrs. Marland was there, attended by two young men, and, a little farther on, he saw old Lord Thrapston tottering along on his stick. Lord Thrapston hated a parson, and scowled at poor Mr. Taylor as he went by. Mr. Taylor shrank from meeting his eye, and hurried along till he reached the Serpentine, where he stood still for a few minutes, drinking in the fresh breeze. But the breeze could not blow the puzzle out of his brain. Was it a crime, or merely an escapade ? What had she said to the young man ? What had her feelings been or become towards the young man ? Moreover, what had she caused the young man's feelings to be for her ? When he came to think it over, Mr. Taylor discovered, with a shock of surprise, that on all these distinctly material points the confession had been singularly incomplete. He was ashamed of this, for, of course, it was his business to make the confession full and exhaustive. He could only plead that, at the moment, it had seemed thorough and candid—an unreserved revelation. Yet those points did, as a fact, remain obscure.

"I wish I knew a little more about human

nature," sighed Mr. Taylor; he was thinking of one division of human nature, and it is likely enough that he knew next to nothing of it.

A hand clapped him on the shoulder, and, with a start, he turned round. A tall young man, in a new frock-coat and a faultless hat, stood by him, smiling at him.

" What, Charlie, old fellow ! " cried Taylor ; " where do you spring from ? "

Charlie explained that he was up in town for a month or two.

"It's splendid to meet you first day! I was going to look you up," he said.

Sigismund Taylor and Charlie had been intimate friends at Oxford, although Charlie was, as time counts there, very considerably the junior. For the last two or three years they had hardly met.

" But what are you up for ? "

" Oh, well, you see, my uncle wants me to get called to the Bar, or something, so I ran up to have a look into it ? "

" Will that take a month ? "

" Look here, old fellow, I've got nothing else to do ; I don't see why I shouldn't stretch it to three months. Besides, I want to spend some time with my ancestors."

" With your ancestors ? "

" In the British Museum ; I'm writing a book about them. Queer lot some of them were, too. Of course I'm specially interested in Agatha Merceron ; but I suppose you never heard of her ? "

Mr. Taylor confessed his ignorance, and Charlie, taking his arm, walked him up and down the bank, while he talked on his pet subject. Agatha Merceron was always interesting, and just now anything about the Pool was interesting ; for there was one reason for his visit to London which he had not disclosed. Nettie Wallace had, when he met her one day, incautiously dropped a word which seemed to imply that the other Agatha was often in London. Nettie tried to recall her words ; but the mischief was done, and Charlie became more than ever convinced that he would grow rusty if he stayed always at Langbury Court. In fact, he could suffer it no longer, and to town he went.

For a long while Sigismund Taylor listened with no more than average interest to Charlie's story, but it chanced that one word caught his notice.

" She comes out of the temple," said Charlie, in the voice of hushed reverence with which he was wont to talk of the unhappy lady.

" Out of where ? " asked Mr. Taylor.

" The temple. Oh, I forgot. The temple is—— " and Charlie gave a description which need not be repeated.

Temple! temple! Where had he heard of a temple lately? Mr. Taylor cudgelled his brains. Why—why—yes, she had spoken of a temple. She said they met in a temple. It was a strange coincidence; the word had struck him at the time. But then everybody knows that, at a certain period, it was common enough to put up these little classical erections as a memorial or merely as an ornament to pleasure grounds. It must be a mere coïncidence. But—— Mr. Taylor stopped short.

" What's up ? " asked Charlie, who had finished his narrative, and was now studying the faces of the ladies who rode past.

" Nothing," answered Mr. Taylor.

And really it was not much ; taken by itself, entirely unworthy of notice ; even taken in conjunction with the temple, of no real significance, that he could see. Still, it was a whimsical thing that, as had just struck him, Charlie's spectre should be named Agatha. But it came to nothing ; how could the name of Charlie's spectre have anything to do with that of his penitent ?

Presently Charlie, too, fell into silence. He beat his stick moodily against his leg and looked glum and absent.

"Ah, well," he said at last, "poor Agatha was hardly used; she paid part of the debt we owe woman."

Mr. Taylor raised his brows, and smiled at this gloomily misogynistic sentiment. He had the perception to grasp in a moment what it indicated. His young friend was, or had lately been, or thought he was likely to be, a lover, and an unhappy one. But he did not press Charlie. Confessions were no luxury to him.

Presently they began to walk back, and Charlie, saying he had to dine with Victor Sutton, made an appointment to see Taylor again, and, leaving him, struck across the Row. Taylor strolled on, and, finding Mrs. Marland still in her seat, sat down by her. She was surprised and pleased to hear that Charlie was in town.

"I left him at home in deep dumps. You've never been to Langbury Court, have you?"

Taylor shook his head.

"Such a sweet old place! But, of course, rather dull for a young man, with nobody but his mother and just one or two slow country neighbours."

" Oh, a run 'll do him good."

" Yes, he was quite moped ; " and Mrs. Marland glanced at her companion. She wanted only a very little encouragement to impart her suspicions to him. It must, in justice to Mrs. Marland, be remembered that she had always found the simplest explanation of Charlie's devotion to the Pool hard to accept, and the most elaborate demonstration of how a Canadian canoe may be upset unconvincing.

" You're a great friend of his, aren't you ? " pursued Mrs. Marland. " So I suppose there's no harm in mentioning my suspicions to you. Indeed I dare say you could be of use to him —I mean, persuade him to be wise. I'm afraid, Mr. Taylor, that he is in some entanglement."

" Dear, dear ! " murmured Mr. Taylor.

" Oh, I've no positive proof, but I fear so— and a very undesirable entanglement, too, with some one quite beneath him. Yes, I think I had better tell you about it."

Mr. Taylor sat silent and, save for a start or two, motionless while his companion detailed her circumstantial evidence. Whether it were enough to prove Mrs. Marland's case or not—whether, that is, it is inconceivable that a young man should go to any place fourteen evenings running, and upset a friend of his youth out of a canoe, except there be a lady involved, is perhaps doubtful; but it was more than enough to show Mr. Sigismund Taylor that the confession he had listened to was based on fact, and that Charlie Merceron was the other party to those stolen interviews, into whose exact degree of heinousness he was now inquiring. This knowledge caused Mr. Taylor to feel that he was in an awkward position.

"Now," asked Mrs. Marland, "candidly, Mr. Taylor, can you suppose anything else than that our friend Charlie was carrying on a very pronounced flirtation with this dressmaker?"

"Dressmaker?"

"Her friend was, and I believe she was too. Something of the kind, anyhow."

"You—you never saw the—the other person?"

"No; she kept out of the way. That looks bad, doesn't it? No doubt she was a tawdry vulgar creature. But a man never notices that!"

At this moment two people were seen approaching. One of them was a man of middle height and perhaps five and thirty years of age; he was stout and thick-built; he had a fat face with bulging cheeks; his eyes were rather like a frog's; he leant very much forward as he walked, and swayed gently from side to side with a rolling swagger; and as his body rolled, his eye rolled too, and he looked this way and that with a jovial leer and a smile of contentment and amusement on his face. The smile and the merry eye redeemed his appearance from blank ugliness, but neither of them indicated a spiritual or exalted mind.

By his side walked a girl, dressed, as Mrs. Marland enviously admitted, as really very few women in London could dress, and wearing, in virtue perhaps of the dress, perhaps of other more precious gifts, an air of assured perfection and dainty disdain. She was listening to her companion's conversation, and did not notice Sigismund Taylor, with whom she was well acquainted.

"Dear me, who are those, I wonder?" exclaimed Mrs. Marland. "She's very *distinguée.*"

"It's Miss Glyn," answered he.

" What ?—Miss Agatha Glyn ? "

" Yes," he replied, wondering whether that little coincidence as to the " Agatha " would suggest itself to any one else.

" Lord Thrapston's granddaughter ? "

" Yes."

" Horrid old man, isn't he ? "

" I know him very slightly."

" And the man—who's he ? "

" Mr. Calder Wentworth."

" To be sure. Why, they're engaged, aren't they ? I saw it in the paper."

" I'm sure I don't know," said Mr. Taylor, in a voice more troubled than the matter seemed to require. " I saw it in the paper too."

" He's no beauty, at any rate; but he's a great match, I suppose ? "

" Oh, perhaps it isn't true."

" You speak as if you wished it wasn't. I've heard about Mr. Wentworth from Victor Sutton—you know who I mean ? " and Mrs. Marland proceeded to give some particulars of Calder Wentworth's career.

Meanwhile that gentleman himself was telling Agatha Glyn a very humorous story. Agatha did not laugh. Suddenly she interrupted him.

" Why don't you ask me more about it ? "

" I thought you'd tell me if you wanted me to know," he answered.

" You are the most insufferable man. Don't you care in the least what I do or where I go ? "

" Got perfect confidence in you," said Calder politely.

" I don't deserve it."

" Oh, I dare say not; but it's so much more comfortable for me."

" I disappeared—simply disappeared—for a fortnight; and you've never asked where I went, or what I did, or—or anything."

" Haven't I ? Where did you go ? "

" I can't tell you."

" There, you see ! What the dickens was the good of my asking ? "

" If you knew what I did I suppose you'd never speak to me again."

" All right. Keep it dark then, please."

" For one thing, I met—— No, I won't."

" I never asked you to, you know."

They walked on a little way in silence.

" Met young Sutton at lunch," observed Calder. " He's been rusticating with some relations of old Van Merceron's. They've got a nice place apparently."

" I particularly dislike Mr. Sutton."

" All right. He shan't come when we're married. Eh ? What ? "

" I didn't speak," said Miss Glyn, who had certainly done something.

" Beg pardon," smiled Calder. " Victor told me rather a joke. It appears there's a young Merceron, and the usual rustic beauty, don't you know—forget the name—but a fat girl, Victor said, and awfully gone on young Merceron. Well, there's a pond or something—— "

" How long will this story last ? " asked Miss Glyn with a tragic air.

" It's an uncommon amusing one," protested Calder. " He upset her in the pond, and—— "

" Do you mind finishing it some other time ? "

" Oh, all right. Thought it 'd interest you."

" It doesn't."

" Never knew such a girl ! No sense of humour ! " commented Calder, with a shake of his head and a backward roll of his eye towards his companion.

But it makes such a difference whether a story is new to the hearer.

CHAPTER VI.

THERE WAS SOMEBODY.

Two worlds and half a dozen industries had conspired to shower gold on Calder Wentworth's head. There was land in the family, brought by his grandmother; there was finance on the paternal side (whence came a Portuguese title, carefully eschewed by Calder); there had been a London street, half a watering-place, a South African mine, and the better part of an American railway. The street and the watering-place remained; the mine and the railway had been sold at the top of the market. About the same time the family name became Wentworth—it had been Stripes, which was felt to be absurd— and the family itself began to take an exalted place in society. The rise was the easier because, when old Mr. Stripes-Wentworth died, young Mr. Calder S. Wentworth became the only representative; and a rich young bachelor can rise lightly to heights inaccessible to the feet of less happily situated folk. It seemed part of Providence's benevolence that when Lady Forteville asked how many " Stripes women " there were, the answer could be " None "; whereupon the Countess at once invited Mr. Calder Wentworth to dinner. Calder went, and rolled his frog's eyes with much amusement when the lady asked him to what Wentworths he belonged ; for, as he observed to Miss Glyn, whom he had the pleasure of escorting, his Wentworths were an entirely new brand, and Lady Forteville knew it as well as if she had read the letters patent and invented the coat-of-arms.

" Mr. Wentworth—Mr. Merceron," said Victor Sutton, with a wave of his hand.

" I believe I know an uncle of yours—an uncommon clever fellow," said Calder, unfolding his napkin and glancing round the dining-room of the Themis Club.

" Oh, Uncle Van ? Yes, we consider him our——"

" Leading article ? Quite so. I've heard a bit about you too—something about a canoe, eh ? "

Charlie looked somewhat disturbed.

" Oughtn't Sutton to have told me ? Well,

it's too late now, because I've told half a dozen fellows."

"But there's nothing to tell."

"Well, I told it to old Thrapston. You don't know him, do you? Cunningest old boy in London. Upon my honour, you know, I shouldn't like to be like old Thrapston, not when I was getting old, you know. He's too——"

"Well, what did he say?" asked Victor.

"He said what you never had the sense to see, my boy; but I expect Mr. Merceron won't be obliged to me for repeating it."

"I should like to hear it," said Charlie, with necessary politeness.

"Well, it's not me, it's old Thrapston; and if you say it's wrong, I'll believe you. Old Thrapston—— Hang it, Victor, that old man ought to be hanged! Why, only the other day I saw him——"

"Do stick to the point," groaned Victor.

"All right. Well, he said, 'I'll lay a guinea there was a——' And he winked his sinful old eye, you know, for all the world like a what-d'ye-call-it on a cathedral—one of those hideous—— I say, what is the word, Victor? I saw 'em when Agatha took me—— Beg pardon, Merceron?"

Was the world full of Agathas? If so, it would be well not to start whenever one was mentioned. Charlie recovered himself.

"I think you must mean a gurgoyle," he said, wondering who this Agatha might be.

"Of course I do. Fancy forgetting that! Gurgoyle, of course. Well, old Thrapston said, 'I'll lay a guinea there was a woman in that dashed summer-house, Calder, my boy.'"

Victor Sutton's eyes lighted with a gleam.

"Well, I'm hanged if I ever thought of that! Charlie, you held us all!"

"Bosh!" said Charlie Merceron. "There was no one there."

"All right. But there ought to have been, you know—to give interest to the position."

"Honour bright, Charlie?" asked Victor Sutton.

"Shut up, Sutton," interposed Calder. "He's not in the Divorce Court. Let's change the subject."

Charlie was in a difficulty, but the better course seemed to be to allow the subject to be changed, in spite of the wink that accompanied Calder's suggestion.

"All right," said Victor. "How is Miss Glyn, Wentworth?"

" Oh, she's all right. She's been in the country for a bit, but she's back now."

" And when is the happy event to be ? "

Calder laid down his knife and fork, and remarked deliberately,

" I haven't, my dear boy, the least idea."

" I should hurry her up," laughed Sutton.

" I'd just like—now I should just like to put you in my shoes for half an hour, and see you hurry up Agatha."

" She couldn't eat me."

" Eat you ? No, but she'd flatten you out so that you'd go under that door and leave room for the jolly draught there is all the same."

Sutton laughed complacently.

" Well, you're a patient man," he observed. " For my part, I like a thing to be off or on."

It came to Charlie Merceron almost as a surprise to find that Victor's impudence—he could call it by no other name—was not reserved for his juniors or for young men from the country; but Calder took it quite good-humouredly, contenting himself with observing,

" Well, it was very soon off in your case, wasn't it, old fellow ? "

Sutton flushed.

" I've told you before that that's not true,"
he said angrily.

Calder laughed.

" All right, all right. We used to think,
once upon a time, Merceron, you know, that
old Victor here was a bit smitten himself;
but he hasn't drugged my champagne yet, so,
of course, as he says, it was all a mistake."

After dinner the three separated. Victor
had to go to a party. Calder Wentworth
proposed to Charlie that they should take a
stroll together with a view to seeing whether,
when they came opposite to the door of a
music-hall, they would "feel like" dropping
in to see part of the entertainment. Charlie
agreed, and, having lit their cigars, they set
out. He found his new friend amusing, and
Calder, for his part, took a liking for Charlie,
largely on account of his good looks; like
many plain people, he was extremely sensitive
to the influence of beauty in women and men
alike.

" I say, old fellow," he said, pressing
Charlie's arm as if he had known him all
his life, " there was somebody in that summer-
house, eh ? "

Charlie turned with a smile and a blush.
He felt confidential.

" Yes, there was, only Victor——"

" Oh, I know. I nearly break his head whenever he mentions any girl I like."

" You know what he'd have thought—and it wasn't anything like that really."

" Who was she, then ? "

" I—I don't know."

" Oh, I don't mean her name, of course. But what was she ? "

" I don't know."

" Where did she come from ? "

" London, I believe."

" Oh ! I say, that's a queer go, Merceron."

" I don't know what to think about it. She's simply vanished," said poor Charlie, and none should wonder that his voice faltered a little. Calder Wentworth laughed at many things, but he did not laugh now at Charlie Merceron. Indeed he looked unusually grave.

" I should drop it," he remarked. "It don't look—well—healthy."

" Ah, you've never seen her," said Charlie.

" No, and I tell you what—it won't be a bad thing if you don't see her again."

" Why ? "

" Because you're just in the state of mind to marry her."

" And why shouldn't I ? "

Mr. Wentworth made no answer, and they walked on till they reached Piccadilly Circus. Then Charlie suddenly darted forward.

" Hallo, what's up ? " cried Calder, following him.

Charlie was talking eagerly to a very smart young lady who had just got down from an omnibus.

" By Jove! he can't have found her ! " thought Calder.

It was not the unknown, but her friend Nettie Wallace, whom Charlie's quick eye had discerned; and the next moment Willie Prime made his appearance. Charlie received them both almost with enthusiasm, and the news from Lang Marsh was asked and given. Calder drew near, and Charlie presented his friends to one another with the intent that he might get a word with Nettie while Calder engrossed her *fiancé's* attention.

" Have—have you heard from Miss Brown lately ? " he was just beginning, when Calder, who had been looking steadily at Nettie, burst out :

" Hallo, I say, Miss Wallace, we've met before, haven't we ? You know me, don't you ? "

Nettie laughed.

"Oh, yes, I know you, sir. You're——"
She paused abruptly, and glanced from Charlie
to Calder, and back from Calder to Charlie.
Then she blushed very red.

"Well, who am I?"

"I—I saw you at—at Miss Glyn's, Mr.
Wentworth."

"'Course you did—that's it;" and, looking
curiously at the girl's flushed face, he added,
"Don't be afraid to mention Miss Glyn; Mr.
Merceron knows all about it."

"All about it, does he, sir?" cried Nettie.
"Well, I'm glad of that. I haven't been easy
in my mind ever since."

Calder's conformation of eye enabled him
to indicate much surprise by facial expression,
and at this moment he used his power to
the full.

"Awfully kind of you, Miss Wallace," said
he, "but I don't see where your responsibility
comes in. Ever since what?"

Nettie shot a glance of inquiry at Charlie,
but here, too, she met only bewilderment.

"Does he know that Miss Glyn is——"
she began.

"Engaged to me? Certainly."

"Oh!"

Willie stood by in silence. He had never heard of this Miss Glyn. Charlie, puzzled as he was, was too intent on Miss Brown to spend much time wondering why Miss Glyn's affairs should have been a trouble to Nettie.

"You'll let me know if you hear about her, won't you?" he asked in a low voice.

Nettie gave up the hope of understanding. She shook her head.

"I'll ask her, if I see her, whether she wishes it," she whispered back; and, with a hasty good night, she seized Willie's arm and hurried him off. Charlie was left alone with Calder.

"What the deuce did she mean?" asked Calder.

"I don't know," answered Charlie.

"Where did you meet her?"

"Oh, down at home. The fellow she was with is a son of a tenant of ours; she's going to marry him."

"She's a nice little girl, but I'm hanged if I know what she meant."

And, as the one was thinking exclusively of Agatha Glyn, and the other spared a thought for no one but Agatha Brown, they did not arrive at an explanation.

One result, however, that chance encounter had. The next morning Miss Agatha Glyn received a letter in the following terms :—

"MADAM,

"I hope you will excuse me intruding, but I think you would wish to know that Mr. Charles Merceron is in London, and that I met him this evening with Mr. Wentworth. As you informed me that you had passed Mr. Merceron on the road two or three times during your visit to Lang Marsh, I think you may wish to be informed of the above. I may add that Mr. Merceron is aware that you are engaged to Mr. Wentworth, but I could not make out how far he was aware of what happened at Lang Marsh. I think he does not know it. Of course you will know whether Mr. Wentworth is aware of your visit there. I should be much obliged if you would be so kind as to tell me *what to say* if I meet the gentlemen again. Mr. Merceron is very pressing in asking me for news of you. I am to be married in a fortnight from the present date,

"And I am, Madam,

"Yours respectfully,

"NETTIE WALLACE."

"In London, and with Calder!" exclaimed Agatha Glyn. "Oh dear! oh dear! oh dear! What is to be done? I wish I'd never gone near the wretched place!"

Then she took up the letter and re-read it.

"He and I mustn't meet, that's all," she said.

Then she slowly tore the letter into very small pieces and put them in the wastepaper basket.

"Calder has no idea where I was," she said, and she sat down by the window and looked out over the Park for nearly ten minutes.

"Ah, well! I should like to see him just once again. Dear old Pool!" said she.

Then she suddenly began to laugh — an action only to be excused in one in her position, and burdened with her sins, by the fact of her having at the moment a peculiarly vivid vision of Millie Bushell going head first out of a canoe.

CHAPTER VII.

THE INEVITABLE MEETING.

THE first Viscount Thrapston had been an eminent public character, and the second a respectable private person; the third had been neither. And yet there was some good in the third. He had loved his only son with a fondness rare to find; and for ten whole years, while the young man was between seventeen and twenty-seven, the old lord lived, for his sake, a life open to no reproach. Then the son died, leaving a lately married wife and a baby-girl, and Lord Thrapston, deprived at once of hope and of restraint, returned to his old courses, till age came upon him and drove him from practice into reminiscence. Mrs. Glyn had outlived her husband fifteen years, and then followed him, fairly snubbed to death, some said, by her formidable father-in-law. The daughter was of sterner stuff, and early discovered for herself that nothing worse than a scowl or a snarl was to be feared. On her, indeed, descended a relic of that tenderness her father had enjoyed, and Agatha used to the full the advantages it gave her. She knew her own importance. It is not every girl who will be a peeress in her own right, and she amused her grandfather by informing him calmly that it was not, on the whole, a subject for regret that she had not been a boy. "You see," said she, " we get rid of the new viscounty, and it's much better to be Warmley than Thrapston."

The fact that she was some day to be " Warmley " was the mainspring of that hair-brained jaunt to Lang Marsh in company with Nettie Wallace. Nettie was the daughter of Lord Thrapston's housekeeper, and the two girls had been intimate in youth, much as Charlie Merceron and Willie Prime had been at the Court; and when Nettie, scorning servitude, set up in life for herself, Agatha gave her her custom, and did not withdraw her friendship. In return she received an allegiance which refused none of her behests, and a regard which abolished all formality between them, except when Nettie got a pen in her hand and set herself to compose a polite letter. The expedition was, of course, to see the Court—the old home of the Warmleys—for which Agatha felt a sentimental attraction. She had told herself that some day, if she were rich (and, Lord Thrapston not being rich, she must have had some other resource in her mind), she would buy back Langbury Court and get rid of the Mercerons altogether. There were only a widow and a boy, she had heard, and they should have their price. So she went to the Court in the businesslike mood of a possible purchaser (Calder could afford anything), as well as in the romantic mood of a girl escaped from everyday surroundings, and plunging into a past full of interest to her. Had not she also read of Agatha Merceron? And in this mixed mood she remained till one evening at the Pool she had met " the boy," when the mood became more mixed still. She dared not now look back on the struggles she had gone through before her meeting with the boy became first a daily event, and then the daily event. She had indulged herself for once. It was not to last; but for once it was overpoweringly sweet to be gazed at by eyes that did not remind her of a frog's, and to see swiftly darting towards her a lithe straight

figure crowned with a head that (so she said)
reminded her of Lord Byron's. But, alas!
alas! why had nobody told her that the boy
was like that before she went? Why did her
grandfather take no care of her? Why did
Calder never show any interest in what she
did? Why, in fine, was everybody so cruel
as to let her do exactly what she liked, and
thereby get into a scrape like this?

One thing was certain. If that boy were
in London, she must avoid him. They must
never meet. It was nonsense for Mr. Sigismund Taylor to talk of making a clean breast
of it—of a dignified apology to Charlie,
coupled with a no less dignified intimation
that their acquaintance must be regarded as
closed. Mr. Taylor knew nothing of the
world. He even wanted her to tell Calder!
No. She was truly and properly penitent, and
she hoped that she received all he said in that
line in a right spirit; but when it came to
a question of expediency, she would rather
have Mrs. Blunt's advice than that of a
thousand Mr. Taylors. So she wrote to Mrs.
Blunt and asked herself to lunch, and Mrs.
Blunt, being an accomplished painstaking
hostess, and having no reason to suppose
that her young friend desired a confidential

interview, at once cast about for some one whom Agatha would like to meet. She did not ask Calder Wentworth—she was not so commonplace as that—but she invited Victor Sutton, and, delighting in a happy flash of inspiration, she added Mr. Vansittart Merceron. The families were connected in some way, she knew, and Agatha certainly ought to know Mr. Merceron.

Accordingly, when Agatha arrived, she found Victor, and she had not been there five minutes before the butler, throwing open the door, announced " Mr. Merceron."

Uncle Van had reached that state of body when he took his time over stairs, and between the announcement and his entrance there was time for Agatha to exclaim, quite audibly,

" Oh ! "

" What's the matter, dear ? " asked Mrs. Blunt; but Uncle Van's entrance forbade a reply, and left Agatha blushing but relieved.

Was she never to hear the end of that awful story ? It might be natural that, her hereditary connection with the Mercerons being disclosed, Mr. Vansittart should discourse of Langbury Court, of the Pool, and of Agatha Merceron ; but was it necessary that Victor Sutton should chime in with the whole history of the canoe and Miss Bushell, or joke with Mr. Merceron about his nephew's "assignations"? The whole topic seemed in bad taste, and she wondered that Mrs. Blunt did not discourage it. But what horrible creatures men were! Did they really think it impossible for a girl to like to talk to a man for an hour or so in the evening without—— ?

"You must let me bring my nephew to meet Miss Glyn," said Uncle Van graciously to his hostess. " She is so interested in the family history that she and Charlie would get on like wildfire. He's mad about it."

"In fact," sniggered Victor (Miss Glyn always detested that man), "so interested that, as you hear, he went to meet Agatha Merceron every evening for a fortnight!"

" You'll be delighted to meet him, won't you, Agatha? We must arrange a day," said Mrs. Blunt.

" Calder knows him," added Victor.

" He's an idle young dog," said Uncle Van, "but a nice fellow. A little flighty and fanciful, as boys will be, but no harm in him. You mustn't attach too much importance to our chaff about his meetings at the Pool, Miss Glyn ; we don't mean any harm."

Agatha tried to smile, but the attempt was

not a brilliant success. She stammered that she would be delighted to meet Mr. Charles Merceron, swearing in her heart that she would sooner start for Tierra del Fuego. But her confession to Mrs. Blunt would save her, if only these odious men would go. They had had their coffee, and their liqueurs, and their cigarettes. What more, in Heaven's name, could even a *man* want to propitiate the god of his idolatry?

Apparently the guests themselves became aware that they were trespassing, for Uncle Van, turning to his hostess with his blandest smile, remarked,

"I hope we're not staying too long. The fact is, my dear Mrs. Blunt, you're always so kind that we took the liberty of telling Calder Wentworth to call for us here. He ought to have come by now."

Mrs. Blunt declared that she would be offended if they thought of going before Calder came. Agatha rose in despair; the confession must be put off. She held out her hand to her hostess. At this moment the door-bell rang.

"That's him," said Victor.

"Sit down again for a minute, dear," urged Mrs. Blunt.

There was renewed hope for the confession. Agatha sat down. But hardly had she done so before the strangest presentiment came over her. She heard the door below open and shut, and it was borne in upon her mind that two men had entered. How she guessed it, she could not tell, but, as she sat there, she had no doubt at all that Charlie Merceron had come with Calder Wentworth. Escape was impossible; but she walked across to the window and stood there, with her back to the door.

"Mr. Wentworth!" she heard, and then, cutting the servant short, came Calder's voice.

"I took the liberty——" he began; and she did not know how he went on, for her head was swimming.

"Agatha! Agatha dear!" called Mrs. Blunt.

Perforce she turned, passing her hand quickly across her brow. Yes, it was so. There he stood by Calder's side, and Calder was saying,

"My dear Agatha, this is Charlie Merceron."

She would not look at Charlie. She moved slowly forward, her eyes fixed on Calder, and bowed with a little set smile. Luckily people pay slight attention to one another's expressions on social occasions, or they must all have noticed her agitation. As it was, only Calder Wentworth looked curiously at her before he turned aside to shake hands with Uncle Van.

Then she felt Charlie Merceron coming nearer, and, a second later, she heard his voice.

"Is it possible that it's you?" he asked in a low tone.

Then she looked at him. His face was pale, and his eyes eagerly straining to read what might be in hers.

"Hush!" she whispered. "Yes. Hush! hush!"

"But—but he told me your name was Glyn?"

"Yes."

"And he says you're engaged to him."

Agatha clasped her hands, and Calder's voice broke in between them,

"Come along, Merceron, we're waiting for you."

"They've got into antiquities already," smiled Mrs. Blunt. "You must come again, Mr. Merceron, and meet Miss Glyn. Mustn't he, Agatha?"

Agatha threw one glance at him.

"If he will," she said.

Charlie pulled himself together, muttered something appropriate, and shuffled out under his uncle's wing. Mr. Vansittart was surprised to find him a trifle confused and awkward in society.

Outside the house, Charlie ranged up beside Calder Wentworth, leaving Uncle Van and Sutton together.

"Well, what do you think of her?" asked Calder.

Charlie gave no opinion. He asked just one question:

"How long have you been engaged to her?"

"How long? Oh, let's see. About—yes, just about a year. I never knew that there was a sort of connection between you and her—sort of relationship, you know. I ain't strong on the Peerage."

"A sort of connection!" There was that in more senses than the one Calder had been told of by Uncle Van. There was a connection that poor Charlie thought Heaven itself had tied on those summer evenings by the Pool, which to strengthen and confirm for ever he had sallied from his home, like a knight in search of his mistress the world over in olden days. And he found her—such as this girl must be! Stay! He did not know all yet. Perhaps she had been forced into a bond she hated. He knew that happened. Did not stories tell of it, and moralists declaim against it? This man—this creature, Calder Wentworth—was buying her with his money, forcing himself on her, brutally capturing her. Of course! How could he have doubted her? Charlie dropped Calder's arm as though it had been made of red-hot iron.

"Hallo!" exclaimed that worthy fellow, unconscious of offence.

Charlie stopped short.

"I can't come," he said. "I—I've remembered an engagement;" and without more he turned away, and shot out of sight round the nearest corner.

"Well, I'm hanged!" said Calder Wentworth, and, with a puzzled frown, he joined his other friends.

CHAPTER VIII.

LEFT alone with Mrs. Blunt, Agatha sank into the nearest chair.

"A very handsome young man, isn't he?" asked the good lady, pushing a chair back into its place. "He'll be an acquisition, I think."

Agatha made no answer, and Mrs. Blunt, glancing at her, found her devouring the carpet with a stony stare.

"What on earth's the matter, child?"

"I'm the wretchedest wickedest girl alive," declared Agatha.

"Good gracious!"

"Mrs. Blunt, who do you think was in the summer-house when Mr. Merceron went there?"

"My dear, are you ill? You jump about so from subject to subject."

"It's all one subject, Mrs. Blunt. There *was* a girl there."

"Well, my dear, and if there was? Boys will be boys; and I'm sure there was no harm."

"No harm! Oh!"

"Agatha, are you crazy?" demanded Mrs. Blunt, with an access of sternness.

"Could I fancy," pursued Agatha, in despairing playfulness mimicking Uncle Van's manner, "how Miss Bushell looked, and how Victor looked, and how everybody looked? Could I fancy it? Why, *I was there!*"

"There! Where?"

"Why, in that wretched little temple. I was the girl, Mrs. Blunt. I—I—I was the milkmaid, as Mr. Sutton says. I was the country wench! Oh dear! oh dear! oh dear!"

Mrs. Blunt, knowing her sex, held out a bottle of salts.

"I'm not mad," said Agatha.

"You're nearly hysterical."

Agatha took a long sniff.

"I think I can tell you now," she said more calmly. "But was ever a girl in such a awful position before?"

It is needless to repeat what Mrs. Blunt said. Her censures will have been long ago anticipated by every right-thinking person, and if she softened them down a little more than strict justice allowed, it must have been because Agatha was an old favourite of hers, and Lord Thrapston an old antipathy. Upon her word, she always wondered that the poor child, brought up by that horrid old man, was not twice as bad as she was.

"But what am I to do about them?" cried Agatha.

"Them" evidently meant Calder and Charlie.

"Do? Why, there's nothing to do. You must just apologize to Mr. Merceron, and tell him that an end had better be put——"

"Oh, I know—Mr. Taylor said that; but, Mrs. Blunt, I don't want an end to be put to our acquaintance. I like him very, very much. Oh, and he thinks me horrid! Oh!"

"Take another sniff," advised Mrs. Blunt. "Of course, if Mr. Merceron is willing to let bygones be bygones, and just be an acquaintance——"

"Oh, but I know he won't. If you knew Charlie——"

"Knew *who*, Agatha?"

"Mr. Merceron," said Agatha in a very humble voice. "If you knew him at all, you'd know he wouldn't do that."

"Then you must send him about his business. Oh, yes, I know. You've treated him atrociously, but Calder Wentworth must be considered first; that is, if you care two straws for the poor fellow, which I begin to doubt."

"Oh, I do, Mrs. Blunt!"

"Agatha, you shameless girl, which of these men—— ?"

"Don't talk as if there were a dozen of them, dear Mrs. Blunt. There are only two."

"One too many."

"Yes, I know. You—you see, I'm—I'm accustomed to Calder."

"Oh, are you?"

"Yes. Don't be unkind, Mrs. Blunt. And then Charlie was something so new—such a charming change—that—— "

"Upon my word, you might be your grandfather. Talk about heredity, and Ibsen, and all that!"

"Can't you help me, dear Mrs. Blunt?"

"I can't give you two husbands, if that's what you want. There, child, don't cry. Never mind me. Have another sniff."

"I shall go home," said Agatha. "Perhaps grandpapa may be able to advise me."

" Your grandfather! Gracious goodness, girl, you're never going to tell him ? "

" Yes, I shall. Grandpapa's had a lot of experience ; he says so."

" I should think he had ! " whispered Mrs. Blunt with uplifted hands.

" Good-bye, Mrs. Blunt. You don't know how unhappy I am. Thanks, yes, a hansom, please. Mrs. Blunt, are you going to ask Mr. Merceron here again ? "

Mrs. Blunt's toleration was exhausted.

" Be off with you ! " she said sternly, pointing a forefinger at the door.

By great good fortune Agatha found Lord Thrapston at home. Drawing a footstool beside his chair, she sat down. Her agitation was past, and she wore a gravely business-like air.

" Grandpapa," she began, " I have got something to tell you."

" Go ahead, my dear," said the old gentle-man, stroking her golden hair. Her father had curls like that when he was a boy.

" Something dreadful I've done, you know. But you won't be very angry, will you ? "

" We'll see."

" You oughtn't to be, because you're not very good yourself, are you ? " and she first glanced up into his burnt-out old eyes and then pressed her lips on his knotted lean old hand.

"Aggy," said he, "I expect you play the deuce with the young fellows, don't you?"

Agatha laughed softly, but a frown succeeded.

"That's just it," she said. "Now, you're to listen and not interrupt, or I shall never be able to manage it. And you're not to look at me, grandpapa."

The narrative—that thrice-told tale—began. As the comments of Mr. Taylor and Mrs. Blunt were omitted, those of Lord Thrapston may well receive like treatment, more especially as they tended not to edification; but before his granddaughter had finished her story the old man had sworn softly four times and chuckled audibly twice.

"I knew there was a girl in that temple, soon as Calder told me," said he.

"But you didn't know who it was. Oh, and Calder doesn't?"

"Not he. Well, you've made a pretty little fool of yourself, missie. What are you going to do now?"

"That's what you've got to tell me."

"I? Oh, I dare say. No, no; you got

into the scrape, and you can get out of it. And "—he suddenly recollected his duties—"look here, Agatha, I must—hang it, Agatha, I shouldn't be doing my duty as—as a grandfather if I didn't say that it's a monstrous disgraceful thing of you to have done. Yes, d——d disgraceful;" and he took a pinch of snuff with an air of severe virtue.

"Yes, dear; but you shouldn't swear, should you?"

Lord Thrapston felt that he had spoilt the moral effect of his reproof, and, without dwelling further on that aspect of the subject, he addressed his mind to the more practical question. The outcome, different as the source was, was the same old verdict.

"We must tell Calder, my dear. It isn't right to keep him in the dark."

"I can't tell him. Why must he be told?"

"Well," said Lord Thrapston, "it's just possible, Aggy, that he may have something to say to it, isn't it?"

"I don't mind what he says," declared Agatha.

"Eh? Why, I thought you were so fond of him."

" So I am."

" And as you're going to marry him—— "

" I never said I was going to marry him. I only said he might be engaged to me, if he liked."

" Oho !   So this young Merceron—— "

" Not at all, grandpapa. Oh, I do wish somebody would help me ! "

Lord Thrapston rose from his seat.

" You must do what you like," he said. " I'm going to tell Calder."

" Oh, why ? "

" Because," he answered, " I'm a man of honour."

Before the impressive invocation of her grandfather's one religion, Agatha's opposition collapsed.

" I suppose he must be told," she admitted mournfully. " I expect he'll never speak to me again, and I'm sure Mr. Merceron won't ; " and she sat on the footstool, the picture of dejection.

Lord Thrapston was moved to enunciate a solemn truth.

" Aggy," said he, shaking his finger at her, " in this world you can't have your fun for nothing." But then he spoilt it by adding regretfully, " More's the pity ! " and off he hobbled to the club, intent on finding Calder Wentworth.

For some time after he went, Agatha sat on her stool in deep thought. Then she rose, sat down at the writing-table, took a pen, and began to bite the end of it. At last she started to write:

"I don't know whether I ought to write or not, but I must tell you how it happened. Oh, don't think too badly of me! I came down just because I had heard so much about the Court, and I wanted to see it, and I came as I did with Nettie Wallace just for fun. I never meant to say I was a dressmaker, you know; but people would ask questions, and I had to say something. I never, never thought of you. I thought you were about fifteen. And you know—oh, you must know—that I met you quite by accident, and was just as surprised as you were. And the rest was all your fault. I didn't want to come again; you know I refused ever so many times; and you promised you wouldn't come if I came, and then you did come. It was really all your fault. And I'm very, very sorry, and you must please try to forgive me, dear Mr. Merceron, and not think me a very wicked girl. I had no idea of coming every evening, but you persuaded me. You know you persuaded me. And how could I tell you I was engaged? You know you never asked me. I would have told you if you had. I am telling Mr. Wentworth all about it, and I don't think you ought to have persuaded me to meet you as you did. It wasn't really kind or nice of you, was it? Because, of course, I'm not very old, and I don't know much about the world, and I never thought of all the horrid things people would say. Do, please, keep this quite a *secret*. I felt I must write you just a line. I wonder what you're thinking about me, or whether you're thinking about me at all. You must never think of me again. I am very, very unhappy, and I do most earnestly hope, dear Mr. Merceron, that I have not made you unhappy. We were both very much to blame, weren't we? But we slipped into it without knowing. Goodbye. I don't think I shall ever forget the dear old Pool, and the temple, and—the rest. But you must please forget me and forgive me. I am very miserable about it, and about everything. I think we had better not know each other any more, so please don't answer this. Just put it in the fire, and think no more about it or me. I wanted to tell you

all this when I saw you to-day, but I couldn't.
Good-bye.   Why did we ever meet?

"AGATHA GLYN."

She read this rather confused composition over twice, growing more sorry for herself each time.   Then she put it in an envelope, addressed it to Charlie, looked out Uncle Van in the Directory, and sent it under cover to his residence.   Then she went and lay down on the hearthrug, and began to cry, and through her tears she said aloud to herself,

" I wonder whether he'll write or come."

Because it seemed to her entirely impossible that, in spite of her prayer, he should put the letter in the fire and let her go.   Surely he, too, remembered the dear old Pool, and the temple, and—the rest!

CHAPTER IX.

TWO MEN OF SPIRIT.

"THE fact is," observed Lord Thrapston complacently, "the girl very much resembles me in disposition."

Calder's eyes grew larger and rounder.

"Do you really think so?" he asked anxiously.

"Well, this little lark of hers—hang me, it's just what I should have enjoyed doing fifty years ago."

"Ah—er—Lord Thrapston, have you noticed the resemblance you speak of in any other way?"

"That girl, except that she is a girl, is myself over again—myself over again."

"The deuce!"

"I beg your pardon, Calder? I grow hard of hearing."

"Nothing, Lord Thrapston. Look here, Lord Thrapston——"

" Well, well, my dear boy ? "

" Oh, nothing ; that is—— "

" But she'll be all right in your hands, my boy. You must keep an eye on her, don't you know. She'll need a bit o' driving ; but I really don't see why you should come to grief. I don't, 'pon my soul. No. With tact on your part, you might very well pull through."

" How d'ye mean tact, Lord Thrapston ? "

" Oh, amuse her. Let her travel ; give her lots of society ; don't bother her with domestic affairs ; don't let her feel she's under any obligation—that's what she kicks against. So do I—always did."

Calder pulled his moustache. Lord Thrapston had briefly sketched the exact opposite of his ideal of married life.

" The fact is," continued the old man, " the boy's an uncommon handsome boy. She can't resist that. No more can I ; never could."

There chanced to be a mirror opposite Calder, and he considered himself impartially. There was, he concluded, every prospect of Miss Glyn resisting any engrossing passion for him.

" It's very good of you to have told me

all about it," he remarked, rising. "I'll think it over."

"Yes, do. Of course, I admit she's given you a perfectly good reason for breaking off your engagement if you like. Mind that. We don't feel aggrieved, Calder. Act as you think best. We admit we're in the wrong, but we must stand by what we've done."

"I shouldn't like to give her any pain——"

"Pain! Oh dear me, no, my dear boy. She won't fret. Make your mind easy about that."

Calder felt a sudden impulse to disclose to Lord Thrapston his secret opinion of him, and he recollected, with a pang, that in the course of so doing he would have to touch on more than one characteristic shared by the old man and Agatha. Where were his visions of a quiet home in the country, of freedom from the irksome duties of society, of an obedient and devoted wife, surrounded by children and flanked by jam-pots? He had once painted this picture for Agatha, shortly after she had agreed to that arrangement which she declined to call a promise of marriage; and it occurred to him now that she had allowed the subject to drop without any expression of concurrence. He took leave of Lord Thrapston, and went for a solitary walk. He wanted to think. But the position of affairs was such that other persons also felt the need of reflection, and Calder had not been walking by the Row very long before, lifting his eyes, he saw a young man approaching. The young man was not attired as he ought to have been; he wore a light suit, a dissolute necktie, and a soft wide-awake crammed down low on his head. He had obviously forsworn the vanities of the world and was wearing the willow. He came up to Calder and held out his hand.

"Wentworth," he said, "I left you rudely the other day. I was doing you an injustice. I have heard the truth from Mrs. Blunt. You are free from all blame. We—we are fellow-sufferers."

His tones were so mournful that Calder shook his hand with warm sympathy, and remarked,

"Pretty rough on us both, ain't it?"

"For me," declared Charlie, "everything is over. My trust in woman is destroyed; my pleasure in life is——"

"Well, I don't feel A1 myself, old chap," said Calder.

"I have written to—to her, to say good-bye."

"No, have you, though?"

"What else could I do? Wentworth, do you suppose that, even if she was free, I would think of her for another moment? Can there be love where there is no esteem, no trust, no confidence?"

"I was just thinking that when you came up," said Calder.

"No, at whatever cost, I—every self-respecting man—must consider first of all what he owes to his name, to his family, to his—Wentworth, to his unborn children."

Calder nodded.

"You, of course," pursued Charlie, "will be guided by your own judgment. As to that, the circumstances seal my lips."

"I don't like it, you know," said Calder.

"As regards you, she may or may not have excuses. I don't know; but she wilfully and grossly deceived me. I have done with her."

"Gad, I believe you're right, Merceron, old chap! A chap ought to stand up for himself, by Jove! You'd never feel safe with her, would you, by Jove?"

"Good-bye," said Charlie suddenly. "I leave Paddington by the 4.15."

"Where are you off to?"

" Hell—I mean home," answered Charlie.

Calder beat his stick against his leg.

" I can't stay here, either," he said moodily.

Charlie stretched out his hand again.

" Come with me," said he.

" Eh ? what ? "

" Come with me ; we'll forget her together."

Calder looked at him.

" Well, you are a good chap. Dashed if I don't. Yes, I will. We'll enjoy ourselves like thunder. But I say, Merceron, I—I ought to write to her, oughtn't I ? "

" I am just going to write myself."

" To—to say good-bye, eh ? "

" Yes."

" I shall write and break it off."

" Come along. We'll go to your rooms and get the thing done, and then catch the train. My luggage is at the station now."

" It won't take me a minute to get mine."

" Wentworth, I'm glad to be rid of her."

" Ah—oh, well—so am I," said Calder.

Late that evening the butler presented Miss Agatha Glyn with two letters on a salver. As her eye fell on the addresses, she started. Her heart began to beat. She sat and looked at the two momentous missives.

" Now, which," she thought, " shall I read

first ? And what shall I do, if they are both obstinate ? "

There was another contingency which Miss Glyn did not contemplate.

After a long hesitation, she took up Charlie's letter, and opened it. It was very short, and began abruptly without any words of address :

" I have received your letter. Your excuses make it worse. I could forgive everything except deceit. I leave London to-day. Good-bye.—C.M."

" Deceit ! " cried Agatha. " How dare he ? What a horrid boy ! "

She was walking up and down the room in a state of great indignation. She had never been talked to like that in her life before. It was ungentlemanly, cruel, brutal. She flung Charlie's letter down on the table angrily.

" I am sure poor dear old Calder won't treat me like that ! " she exclaimed, taking up his letter.

It ran thus—

" My dear Agatha,

" I hope you will believe that I write this without any feeling of anger towards you. My regard for you remains very great, and I hope we shall always be very good friends; but, after long and careful consideration, I have come to the conclusion that the story Lord Thrapston told me shows conclusively what I have been fearing for some time past—namely, that I have not been so lucky as to win a real affection from you, and that we are not likely to make one another happy. Therefore, thanking you very much for your kindness in the past, I think I had better restore your liberty to you. I shall hear with very great pleasure of your happiness. I leave town to-day for a little while, in order that you may not be exposed to the awkwardness of meeting me.

"Always yours most sincerely,

"CALDER WENTWORTH."

Agatha passed her hand across her brow; then she re-read Calder's letter, and then Charlie's. Yes, there was not the least doubt about it! Both of the gentlemen had—well, what they had done did not admit of being put into tolerable words. With a little shriek Agatha flung herself on the sofa.

The door opened, and Lord Thrapston entered.

"Well, Aggy, what's the news? Still

bothered by your two young men? Hallo! what's wrong?"

"Read them!" cried Agatha, with a gesture towards the table.

"Eh? Read what? Oh, I see!"

He sat down at the table and put on his glasses. Agatha turned her face towards the wall; for her also everything was over. For a time no sound was audible save an occasional crackle of the note-paper in Lord Thrapston's shaking fingers. Then, to Agatha's indescribable indignation, there came another sort of crackle—a dry, grating, derisive chuckle—from that flinty-hearted old man, her grand-father.

"Good, monstrous good, 'pon my life!" said he.

"You're laughing at me!" she cried, leaping up.

"Well, my dear, I'm afraid I am."

"Oh, how cruel men are!"

"H'm! They're both men of spirit, evidently."

"Calder I can just understand. I—perhaps I did treat Calder rather badly——"

"Oh, you go so far as to admit that, do you, Aggy?"

"But Charlie! Oh, to think that Charlie

should treat me like that!" and she threw herself on the sofa again.

Lord Thrapston sat quite still. Presently Agatha rose, came to the table, and took up her two letters. She looked at them both; and the old man, seeming to notice nothing, yet kept his eye on her.

"I shall destroy these things," said she; and she tore Calder's letter into tiny fragments, and flung them on the fire. Charlie's she crumpled up and held in her hand.

"Good night, grandpapa," she said wearily, and kissed him.

"Good night, my dear," he answered.

And, whatever she did when she went upstairs, Lord Thrapston was in a position to swear that Charlie's letter was not destroyed in the drawing-room.

CHAPTER X.

THE INCARNATION OF LADY AGATHA.

" She's such a dear good girl, Mr. Wentworth," said Lady Merceron. " She's the greatest comfort I have."

It was after luncheon at Langbury Court. Lady Merceron and Calder sat on the lawn; Mrs. Marland and Millie Bushell were walking up and down; Charlie was lying in a hammock. A week had passed since the two young men had startled Lady Merceron by their unexpected arrival, and since then the good lady had been doing her best to entertain them; for, as she could not help noticing, they seemed a little dull. It was a great change from the whirl of London to the deep placidity of the Court, and Lady Merceron could not quite understand why Charlie had tired so soon of his excursion, or why his friend persisted with so much fervour that anything was better than London, and the Court the most charming place he had ever seen. Of the two Charlie seemed to feel the *ennui* much the more severely. Yet, while Mr. Wentworth spoke of returning to town in a few weeks, Charlie asseverated that he had paid his last visit to that revolting and disappointing place. Lady Merceron wished she had Uncle Van by her side to explain these puzzling inconsistencies. However there was a bright side to the affair: the presence of the young men was a godsend to poor Millie, who, by reason of the depressed state of agriculture, had been obliged this year to go without her usual six weeks of London in the season.

" And she never grumbles about it," said Lady Merceron admiringly. " She looks after her district, and takes a ride, and plays tennis, when she can get a game, poor girl, and is always cheerful and happy. She'd be a treasure of a wife to any man."

" You'd better persuade Charlie of that, Lady Merceron."

" Oh, Charlie never thinks of such a thing as marrying. He thinks of nothing but his antiquities."

" Doesn't he ? " asked Calder, with apparent sympathy and a covert sad amusement.

"Mr. Wentworth," said Mrs. Marland, approaching, "I believe it's actually a fact that you've been here a week and have never yet been to the Pool."

At this fateful word Calder looked embarrassed, Charlie raised his head from the hammock, and Millie glanced involuntarily towards him.

"We must take you," pursued Mrs. Marland, "this very evening. "You'll come, Miss Bushell?"

"I don't think I care very much about the Pool," said Millie.

"We won't let Mr. Merceron take you in his canoe this time."

Charlie rolled out of the hammock and came up to them.

"You must take us to the Pool. I don't believe you've been there since you came back. Poor Agatha will quite——"

"Agatha!" exclaimed Calder.

"Agatha Merceron, you know. Why, haven't you heard——?"

"Oh, ah! Yes, of course. I beg your pardon."

"I hate that beastly Pool," said Charlie.

"How can you?" smiled Mrs. Marland. "You used to spend hours there every evening."

Charlie glanced uneasily at Calder, who turned very red.

"Times have changed, have they?" Mrs. Marland asked archly. "You've got tired of looking in vain for Agatha?"

"Oh, all right," said Charlie crossly, "we'll go after tea."

Anything seemed better than this rallying mood of Mrs. Marland's.

Presently the two young men went off together to play a game at billiards; but after half a dozen strokes Charlie plumped down in a chair.

"I say, Calder, old chap, how do *you* feel?" he asked.

Calder licked his cigar meditatively.

"Better," said he at last.

"Oh!"

"And you?"

"Worse—worse every day. I can't stand it, old chap. I shall go back."

"What, to her?"

"Yes."

"That's hardly sticking to our bargain, you know."

"But, hang it, what's the good of our both cutting her?"

"Oh, I thought you did it because you

were disgusted with her. That was my reason."

" So it was mine, but—— "

" Probably she's got some other fellow by now," observed Calder calmly.

" The devil ! " cried Charlie. " What makes you think so ? "

" Oh, nothing. I know her way, you see."

" You think she's that sort of girl ? Good Heavens ! "

" Well, if she wasn't, I'd like to know where you'd be, my friend. I shouldn't have the honour of your acquaintance."

Charlie ignored this point.

" And yet you wanted to marry her ? "

" I dare say I was an ass—like better men before me—and—er—since me."

" Hang it ! " cried Charlie. " I'm sick of the whole thing. I'm sick of life. I'm sick of all the nonsense of it. For two straws I'd have done with it, and marry Millie Bushell."

" What ! Look here, Charlie—— "

Calder left his sentence unfinished.

" Well ? " said Charlie.

" If," said Calder slowly, " there are any girls, either down here or in London, whom you're quite sure you'll never want to marry,

I should like to be introduced to one of 'em, Charlie, if you've no objections."

" What do you mean ? "

" Why, in fact, during this last week, Charlie, I have come to have a great esteem for Miss Bushell. There's about her a something—a solidity—— "

" She can't help that, poor girl."

" A solidity of mind," said Calder, a little stiffly.

" Oh, I beg pardon. But I say, Calder, what are you driving at ? "

" Charlie ! Charlie ! " sounded from outside. " Tea's ready."

Calder rose and took Charlie by the arm.

" Should I be safe," he asked solemnly, " in allowing myself to fall in love with Miss Bushell, or are you likely to step in again ? "

" You mean it ? Honour bright, Calder ? "

" Yes."

" Where's Bradshaw ? By Jove, where's Bradshaw ? "

" Bradshaw ? What the devil has Bradshaw—— ? "

" Why, a train, man—a train to town."

" I don't want to go to town, bless the man—— "

" You !   No, but I do.   To town, Calder—
to Agatha, you old fool."

" Oh, that's your lay ? "

" Yes, of course.   I couldn't go back on
you, but if you're off—— "

" Charlie, old fellow, think again."

" Go to the deuce !   Where's that—— ? "

" Charlie, Charlie !   Tea ! "

" Hang tea ! " he cried ; but Calder dragged
him off, telling him that to-morrow would do
for Bradshaw.

At tea Charlie's spirits were very much
better, and it was observed that Calder Wentworth paid marked attention to Millie Bushell,
so that, when they started for the Pool, Millie
was prevailed upon to be one of the party, on
the understanding that Mr. Wentworth would
take care of her.   This time the expedition
went off more quietly than it had previously,
but at the last moment the ladies declared that
they would be late for dinner if they waited
till it was time for Agatha Merceron to come.

" Oh, nonsense ! " said Calder.   " Come
over to the temple, Miss Bushell.   I won't
upset the canoe."

" Well, if you insist," said Millie.

Then Mrs. Marland remarked, in the quiet-
est voice in the world,

" There's some one in the temple."

" What ? " cried Millie.

" Eh ? " exclaimed Calder.

" Nonsense ! " said Charlie.

" I saw a face at the window," insisted Mrs. Marland.

" Oh, Mrs. Marland ! Was it very awful ? "

" Not at all, Millie—very pretty," and she gave Charlie a look full of meaning.

" Look, look ! " cried Millie, in strong agitation.

And, as they looked, a slim figure in white came quietly out of the temple, a smile—and, alas ! no vestige of a blush—on her face, walked composedly down the steps, and, standing on the lowest one, thence—did not throw herself into the water—but called, in the most natural voice in the world,

" Which of you is coming to fetch me ? "

Charlie looked at Calder. Calder said,

" I think you'd better put her across, old man. And—er—we might as well walk on."

They turned away, Millie's eyes wide in surprise, Mrs. Marland smiling the smile of triumphant sagacity.

" I was coming to you to-morrow," cried Charlie, the moment his canoe bumped against the steps.

"What do you mean, sir, by staying away a whole week? How could you?"

"I don't know," said Charlie. "You see, I couldn't come till Calder——"

"Oh, what about Calder?"

"He's all right."

"What? Miss—the girl you upset out of the canoe?"

"I think so," said Charlie.

"Ah, well!" said Agatha. "But how very curious!" Then she smiled at Charlie, and asked,

"But what love can there be, Mr. Merceron, where there is deceit?"

Charlie took no notice at all of this question.

"Do you mind Calder going?" he whispered.

"Well, not much," said Miss Glyn. Thus it was that the barony of Warmley returned to the house of Merceron, and the portrait of the wicked lord came to hang once more in the dining-room. So the curtain falls on the comedy; and what happened afterwards behind the scenes, whether another comedy, or a tragedy, or a mixed half-and-half sort of entertainment, now grave, now gay, sometimes perhaps delightful, and again of tempered charm—why, as to all this, what reck the spectators who are crowding out of the theatre and home to bed?

But it seems as if, in spite of certain drawbacks in Agatha Merceron's character, nothing very dreadful can have happened, because Mr. and Mrs. Wentworth, who are very particular folk, went to stay at the Court the other day, and their only complaint was that Charlie and his bride were always at the Pool!

And, for his own part, if he may be allowed a word (which some people say he ought not to be) here, just at the end, the writer begs to say that he once knew Agatha, and—he would have taken the risks. However, a lady to whom he has shown this history differs entirely from him, and thinks that no sensible man would have married her. But, then, that is not the question.

THE PHILOSOPHER IN THE APPLE ORCHARD.

It was a charmingly mild and balmy day. The sun shone beyond the orchard, and the shade was cool inside. A light breeze stirred the boughs of the old apple tree under which the philosopher sat. None of these things did the philosopher notice, unless it might be when the wind blew about the leaves of the large volume on his knees, and he had to find his place again. Then he would exclaim against the wind, shuffle the leaves till he got the right page, and settle to his reading. The book was a treatise on ontology; it was written by another philosopher, a friend of this philosopher's; it bristled with fallacies, and this philosopher was discovering them all, and noting them on the fly-leaf at the end. He was not going to review the book (as some might have thought from his behaviour), or even to answer it in a work of his own. It was just that he found a pleasure in stripping any poor fallacy naked and crucifying it.

Presently a girl in a white frock came into the orchard. She picked up an apple, bit it, and found it ripe. Holding it in her hand, she walked up to where the philosopher sat, and looked at him. He did not stir. She took a bite out of the apple, munched it, and swallowed it. The philosopher crucified a fallacy on the fly-leaf. The girl flung the apple away.

"Mr. Jerningham," said she, "are you very busy?"

The philosopher, pencil in hand, looked up.

"No, Miss May," said he, "not very."

"Because I want your opinion."

"In one moment," said the philosopher apologetically.

He turned back to the fly-leaf, and began to nail the last fallacy a little tighter to the cross. The girl regarded him, first with amused impatience, then with a vexed frown, finally with a wistful regret. He was so very old for his age, she thought; he could not be much beyond thirty; his hair was thick and full of waves, his eyes bright and clear, his complexion not yet divested of all youth's relics.

"Now, Miss May, I'm at your service," said the philosopher, with a lingering look at his impaled fallacy. And he closed the book, keeping it, however, on his knee.

The girl sat down just opposite to him.

"It's a very important thing I want to ask you," she began, tugging at a tuft of grass, "and it's very—difficult, and you mustn't tell any one I asked you; at least, I'd rather you didn't."

"I shall not speak of it; indeed, I shall probably not remember it," said the philosopher.

"And you mustn't look at me, please, while I'm asking you."

"I don't think I was looking at you, but if I was I beg your pardon," said the philosopher apologetically.

She pulled the tuft of grass right out of the ground and flung it from her with all her force.

"Suppose a man——" she began. "No, that's not right."

"You can take any hypothesis you please," observed the philosopher, "but you must verify it afterwards, of course."

"Oh, do let me go on. Suppose a girl, Mr. Jerningham—— I wish you wouldn't nod."

"It was only to show that I followed you."

"Oh, of course you 'follow me,' as you call it. Suppose a girl had two lovers—you're nodding again!—or, I ought to say, suppose there were two men who might be in love with a girl."

"Only two?" asked the philosopher. "You see, any number of men *might* be in love with—— "

"Oh, we can leave the rest out," said Miss May, with a sudden dimple; "they don't matter."

"Very well," said the philosopher. "If they are irrelevant we will put them aside."

"Suppose, then, that one of these men was, oh, *awfully* in love with the girl, and—and proposed, you know—— "

"A moment!" said the philosopher, opening a note-book. "Let me take down his proposition. What was it?"

"Why, proposed to her—asked her to marry him," said the girl, with a stare.

"Dear me! How stupid of me! I forgot that special use of the word. Yes?"

" The girl likes him pretty well, and her people approve of him, and all that, you know."

" That simplifies the problem," said the philosopher, nodding again.

" But she's not in—in love with him, you know. She doesn't *really* care for him—*much.* Do you understand ? "

" Perfectly. It is a most natural state of mind."

" Well, then, suppose that there's another man—— What are you writing ? "

" I only put down (B)—like that," pleaded the philosopher, meekly exhibiting his note-book.

She looked at him in a sort of helpless exasperation, with just a smile somewhere in the background of it.

" Oh, you really are——! " she exclaimed. " But let me go on. The other man is a friend of the girl's; he's very clever—oh, fearfully clever; and he's rather handsome. You needn't put that down."

" It *is* certainly not very material," admitted the philosopher, and he crossed out " handsome." " Clever " he left.

" And the girl is most awfully—she admires him tremendously; she thinks him just the greatest man that ever lived, you know. And she—she——" The girl paused.

"I'm following," said the philosopher, with pencil poised.

"She'd think it better than the whole world if—if she could be anything to him, you know."

"You mean become his wife?"

"Well, of course I do—at least I suppose I do."

"You spoke rather vaguely, you know."

The girl cast one glance at the philosopher as she replied,

"Well, yes. I did mean become his wife."

"Yes. Well?"

"But," continued the girl, starting on another tuft of grass, "he doesn't think much about those things. He likes her. I think he likes her——"

"Well, doesn't dislike her?" suggested the philosopher. "Shall we call him indifferent?"

"I don't know. Yes, rather indifferent. I don't think he thinks about it, you know. But she—she's pretty. You needn't put that down."

"I was not about to do so," observed the philosopher.

"She thinks life with him would be just

heaven; and—and she thinks she would make him awfully happy. She would—would be so proud of him, you see."

" I see. Yes? "

" And—I don't know how to put it, quite—she thinks that if he ever thought about it at all, he might care for her; because he doesn't care for anybody else; and she's pretty—— "

" You said that before."

" Oh, dear, I dare say I did. And most men care for somebody, don't they?—some girl, I mean."

" Most men, no doubt," conceded the philosopher.

" Well, then, what ought she to do? It's not a real thing, you know, Mr. Jerningham. It's in—in a novel I was reading." She said this hastily, and blushed as she spoke.

" Dear me! And it's quite an interesting case! Yes, I see. The question is, Will she act most wisely in accepting the offer of the man who loves her exceedingly, but for whom she entertains only a moderate affection—— "

" Yes. Just a liking. He's just a friend."

" Exactly. Or in marrying the other whom she loves ex—— "

" That's not it. How can she marry him? He hasn't—he hasn't asked her, you see."

"True.   I forgot.   Let us assume, though, for the moment, that he has asked her.   She would then have to consider which marriage would probably be productive of the greater sum total of—— "

" Oh, but you needn't consider that."

" But it seems the best logical order.   We can afterwards make allowance for the element of uncertainty caused by—— "

"Oh, no.   I don't want it like that.   I know perfectly well which she'd do if he—the other man, you know—asked her."

" You apprehend that—— ? "

" Never mind what I ' apprehend.'   Take it just as I told you."

" Very good.   A has asked her hand, B has not."

" Yes."

" May I take it that, but for the disturbing influence of B, A would be a satisfactory—er —candidate ? "

" Ye—es.   I think so."

" She therefore enjoys a certainty of considerable happiness if she marries A ? "

" Ye—es.   Not perfect, because of—B, you know."

" Quite so, quite so ; but still a fair amount of happiness.   Is it not so ? "

"I don't—well, perhaps."

"On the other hand, if B did ask her, we are to postulate a higher degree of happiness for her?"

"Yes, please, Mr. Jerningham — much higher."

"For both of them?"

"For her. Never mind him."

"Very well. That again simplifies the problem. But his asking her is a contingency only?"

"Yes, that's all."

The philosopher spread out his hands.

"My dear young lady," he said, "it becomes a question of degree. How probable or improbable is it?"

"I don't know. Not very probable—unless —unless—— "

"Well?"

"Unless he did happen to notice, you know."

"Ah, yes. We supposed that, if he thought of it, he would probably take the desired step —at least, that he might be led to do so. Could she not—er—indicate her preference?"

"She might try—no, she couldn't do much. You see, he—he doesn't think about such things."

"I understand precisely. And it seems to me, Miss May, that in that very fact we find our solution."

"Do we?" she asked.

"I think so. He has evidently no natural inclination towards her—perhaps not towards marriage at all. Any feeling aroused in him would be necessarily shallow and in a measure artificial—and in all likelihood purely temporary. Moreover, if she took steps to arouse his attention, one of two things would be likely to happen. Are you following me?"

"Yes, Mr. Jerningham."

"Either he would be repelled by her overtures—which you must admit is not improbable—and then the position would be unpleasant, and even degrading, for her; or, on the other hand, he might, through a misplaced feeling of gallantry——"

"Through what?"

"Through a mistaken idea of politeness, or a mistaken view of what was kind, allow himself to be drawn into a connection for which he had no genuine liking. You agree with me that one or other of these things would be likely?"

"Yes, I suppose they would, unless he did come to care for her."

"Ah, you return to that hypothesis. I think it's an extremely fanciful one. No. She needn't marry A, but she must let B alone."

The philosopher closed his book, took off his glasses, wiped them, replaced them, and leaned back against the trunk of the apple tree. The girl picked a dandelion in pieces. After a long pause she asked,

"You think B's feelings wouldn't be at all likely to—to change?"

"That depends on the sort of man he is. But if he is an able man, with intellectual interests which engross him—a man who has chosen his path in life—a man to whom women's society is not a necessity——"

"He's just like that," said the girl, and she bit the head off a daisy.

"Then," said the philosopher, "I see not the least reason for supposing that his feelings will change."

"And would you advise her to marry the other—A?"

"Well, on the whole, I should. A is a good fellow (I think we made A a good fellow): he is a suitable match, his love for her is true and genuine——"

"It's tremendous!"

"Yes—and—er—extreme. She likes him.

There is every reason to hope that her liking will develop into a sufficiently deep and stable affection.   She will get rid of her folly about B, and make A a good wife.   Yes, Miss May, if I were the author of your novel, I should make her marry A, and I should call that a happy ending."

A silence followed.   It was broken by the philosopher.

"Is that all you wanted my opinion about, Miss May?" he asked, with his finger between the leaves of the treatise on ontology.

"Yes, I think so.   I hope I haven't bored you?"

"I've enjoyed the discussion extremely.   I had no idea that novels raised points of such psychological interest.   I must find time to read one."

The girl had shifted her position till, instead of her full face, her profile was turned towards him.   Looking away towards the paddock that lay brilliant in sunshine on the skirts of the apple orchard, she asked, in low slow tones, twisting her hands in her lap,

"Don't you think that perhaps if B found out afterwards—when she had married A, you know—that she had cared for him so very, very much, he might be a little sorry?"

" If he were a gentleman, he would regret
it deeply."

" I mean—sorry on his own account ; that
—that he had thrown away all that, you
know ? "   .

The Professor looked meditative.

" I think," he pronounced, " that it is very
possible he would.   I can well imagine it."

" He might never find anybody to love him
like that again," she said, gazing on the
gleaming paddock.

" He probably would not," agreed the
philosopher.

" And—and most people like being loved,
don't they ? "

" To crave for love is an almost universal
instinct, Miss May."

" Yes, almost," she said, with a dreary
little smile. " You see, he'll get old and—
and have no one to look after him."

" He will."

" And no home."

" Well, in a sense, none," corrected the
philosopher, smiling.   " But   really   you'll
frighten me. I'm a bachelor myself, you
know, Miss May."

" Yes," she whispered just audibly.

" And all your terrors are before me."

T

" Well, unless——"

" Oh, we needn't have that ' unless,' ' laughed the philosopher cheerfully. " There's no ' unless ' about it, Miss May."

The girl jumped to her feet ; for an instant she looked at the philosopher. She opened her lips as if to speak, and, at the thought of what lay at her tongue's tip, her face grew red. But the philosopher was gazing past her, and his eyes rested in calm contemplation on the gleaming paddock.

" A beautiful thing, sunshine, to be sure," said he.

Her blush faded away into paleness ; her lips closed. Without speaking, she turned and walked slowly away, her head drooping. The philosopher heard the rustle of her skirt in the long grass of the orchard ; he watched her for a few moments.

" A pretty graceful creature," said he with a smile. Then he opened his book, took his pencil in his hand, and slipped in a careful forefinger to mark the flyleaf.

The sun had passed mid-heaven, and began to decline westwards before he finished the book. Then he stretched himself and looked at his watch.

" Good gracious, two o'clock ! I shall be

late for lunch!" and he hurried to his feet.

He was very late for lunch.

"Everything's cold," wailed his hostess. "Where have you been, Mr. Jerningham?"

"Only in the orchard—reading."

"And you've missed May!"

"Missed Miss May? How do you mean? I had a long talk with her this morning—a most interesting talk."

"But you weren't here to say good-bye. Now, you don't mean to say that you forgot that she was leaving by the two o'clock train? What a man you are!"

"Dear me! To think of my forgetting it!" said the philosopher shamefacedly.

"She told me to say good-bye to you for her."

"She's very kind. I can't forgive myself."

His hostess looked at him for a moment; then she sighed, and smiled, and sighed again.

"Have you everything you want?" she asked.

"Everything, thank you," said he, sitting down opposite the cheese, and propping his book (he thought he would just run through the last chapter again) against the loaf; "everything in the world that I want, thanks."

His hostess did not tell him that the girl had come in from the apple-orchard, and run hastily upstairs, lest her friend should see what her friend did see in her eyes. So that he had no suspicion at all that he had received an offer of marriage—and refused it. And he did not refer to anything of that sort when he paused once in his reading and exclaimed:

" I'm really sorry I missed Miss May. That was an interesting case of hers. But I gave the right answer. The girl ought to marry A."

And so the girl did.

THE CURATE OF POLTONS.

I MUST confess at once that at first, at least, I very much admired the Curate. I am not referring to my admiration of his fine figure— six feet high and straight as an arrow—nor of his handsome, open, ingenuous countenance, or his candid blue eye, or his thick curly hair. No; what won my heart from an early period of my visit to my cousins, the Poltons of Poltons Park, was the fervent, undisguised, unashamed, confident, and altogether matter-of-course manner in which he made love to Miss Beatrice Queenborough, only daughter and heiress of the wealthy shipowner, Sir Wagstaff Queenborough, Bart., and Eleanor his wife. It was purely the manner of the Curate's advances that took my fancy; in the mere fact of them there was nothing re-markable. All the men in the house (and a good many outside) made covert, stealthy, and indirect steps in the same direction ; for Trix (as her friends called her) was, if not wise, at least pretty and witty, displaying to the material eye a charming figure, and to the mental a delicate heartlessness—both attributes which challenge a self-respecting man's best efforts. But then came the fatal obstacle. From heiresses in reason a gentleman need neither shrink nor let himself be driven ; but when it comes to something like twenty thousand a year—the reported amount of Trix's *dot*—he distrusts his own motives almost as much as the lady's relatives distrust them for him. We all felt this—Stanton, Rippleby, and I ; and, although I will not swear that we spoke no tender words and gave no meaning glances, yet we reduced such concessions to natural weakness to a minimum, not only when Lady Queenborough was by, but at all times. To say truth, we had no desire to see our scalps affixed to Miss Trix's pretty belt, nor to have our hearts broken (like that of the young man in the poem) before she went to Homburg in the autumn.

With the Curate it was otherwise. He— Jack Ives, by the way, was his name—appeared to rush, not only upon his fate, but in the face of all possibility and of Lady Queenborough. My cousin and hostess, Dora Polton, was very much distressed about him. She said that he was such a nice young fellow, and that it was a great pity to see him preparing such unhappiness for himself. Nay, I happen to know that she spoke very seriously to Trix, pointing out the wickedness of trifling with him; whereupon Trix, who maintained a bowing acquaintance with her conscience, avoided him for a whole afternoon, and endangered all Algy Stanton's prudent resolutions by taking him out in the Canadian canoe. This demonstration in no way perturbed the Curate. He observed that, as there was nothing better to do, we might as well play billiards, and proceeded to defeat me in three games of a hundred up (no, it is quite immaterial whether we played for anything or not); after which he told Dora that the Vicar was taking the evening service—it happened to be the day when there was one at the parish church—a piece of information only relevant in so far as it suggested that Mr. Ives could accept an invitation to dinner if one were proffered to him. Dora, very weakly, rose to the bait; Jack Ives, airily remarking that there was no use in ceremony

among friends, seized the place next to Trix
at dinner (her mother was just opposite) and
walked on the terrace after dinner with her
in the moonlight.   When the ladies retired
he came into the smoking-room, drank a
whisky-and-soda, said that Miss Queenborough
was really a very charming companion, and
apologised for leaving us early on the ground
that his sermon was still unwritten.   My
good cousin, the Squire, suggested rather
grimly that a discourse on the vanity of
human wishes might be appropriate.

"I shall preach," said Mr. Ives thoughtfully, "on the opportunities of wealth."

This resolution he carried out on the next
day but one, that being a Sunday.   I had the
pleasure of sitting next to Miss Trix, and I
watched her with some interest as Mr. Ives
developed his theme.   I will not try to reproduce the sermon, which would have seemed
by no means a bad one, had any of our party
been able to ignore the personal application
which we read into it: for its main burden
was no other than this—that wealth should
be used by those who were fortunate enough
to possess it (here Trix looked down and
fidgeted with her Prayer-book) as a means of
promoting greater union between themselves,

and the less richly endowed, and not—as,
alas ! had too often been the case—as though
it were a new barrier set up between them
and their fellow-creatures. (Here Miss Trix
blushed slightly and had recourse to her
smelling-bottle.) " You," said the Curate,
waxing rhetorical as he addressed an im-
aginary, but bloated, capitalist, " have no
more right to your money than I have. It
is entrusted to you to be shared with me."
At this point I heard Lady Queenborough sniff,
and Algy Stanton snigger. I stole a glance
at Trix and detected a slight waver in the
admirable lines of her mouth.

" A very good sermon, didn't you think ? "
I said to her, as we walked home.

" Oh, very," she replied demurely.

" Ah, if we followed all we heard in
church ! " I sighed.

Miss Trix walked in silence for a few yards.
By dint of never becoming anything else, we
had become very good friends ; and presently
she remarked, quite confidentially,

" He's very silly, isn't he ? "

" Then you ought to snub him," said I
severely.

" So I do—sometimes. He's rather amusing, though."

" Of course, if you're prepared to make the sacrifice involved—— "

" Oh, what nonsense ! "

" Then you've no business to amuse yourself with him."

" Dear, dear ! how moral you are ! " said Trix.

The next development in the situation was this : My cousin Dora received a letter from the Marquis of Newhaven, with whom she was acquainted, praying her to allow him to run down to Poltons for a few days ; he reminded her that she had once given him a general invitation : if it would not be inconvenient— and so forth.   The meaning of this communication did not, of course, escape my cousin, who had witnessed the writer's attentions to Trix in the preceding season ; nor did it escape the rest of us (who had talked over the said attentions at the club) when she told us about it, and announced that Lord'Newhaven would arrive in the middle of next day. Trix affected dense unconsciousness ; her mother allowed herself a mysterious smile—which, however, speedily vanished when the Curate (he was taking lunch with us) observed in a cheerful tone :

" Newhaven ? Oh, I remember the chap at

the House—ploughed twice in Smalls—stumpy fellow, isn't he? Not a bad chap, though, you know, barring his looks. I'm glad he's coming."

"You won't be soon, young man," Lady Queenborough's angry eye seemed to say.

"I remember him," pursued Jack, "awfully smitten with a tobacconist's daughter in the Corn—oh, it's all *right*, Lady Queenborough—she wouldn't look at him."

This quasi-apology was called forth by the fact of Lady Queenborough pushing back her chair and making for the door. It did not at all appease her to hear of the scorn of the tobacconist's daughter. She glared sternly at Jack, and disappeared. He turned to Trix and reminded her — without diffidence and *coram populo*, as his habit was—that she had promised him a stroll in the west wood.

What happened on that stroll I do not know; but meeting Miss Trix on the stairs later in the afternoon, I ventured to re-mark,

"I hope you broke it to him gently, Miss Queenborough?"

"I don't know what you mean," replied Trix haughtily.

"You were out nearly two hours," said I.

"Were we?" asked Trix with a start. "Good gracious! Where was mamma, Mr. Wynne?"

"On the lawn—watch in hand."

Miss Trix went slowly upstairs, and there is not the least doubt that something serious passed between her and her mother, for both of them were in the most atrocious of humours that evening; fortunately the curate was not there. He had a Bible-class.

The next day Lord Newhaven arrived. I found him on the lawn when I strolled out, after a spell of letter-writing, about four o'clock. Lawn tennis was the order of the day, and we were all in flannels.

"Oh, here's Mark," cried Dora, seeing me. "Now, Mark, you and Mr. Ives had better play against Trix and Lord Newhaven. That'll make a very good set."

"No, no, Mrs. Polton," said Jack Ives. "They wouldn't have a chance. Look here, I'll play with Miss Queenborough against Lord Newhaven and Wynne."

Newhaven—whose appearance, by the way, though hardly distinguished, was not quite so unornamental as the curate had led us to expect—looked slightly displeased, but Jack gave him no time for remonstrance. He whisked Trix off, and began to serve all in a moment. I had a vision of Lady Queenborough approaching from the house with face aghast. The set went on; and, owing entirely to Newhaven's absurd chivalry in sending all the balls to Jack Ives instead of following the well-known maxim to "pound away at the lady," they beat us. Jack wiped his brow, strolled up to the tea-table with Trix, and remarked in exultant tones,

"We make a perfect couple, Miss Queenborough; we ought never to be separated."

Dora did not ask the Curate to dinner that night, but he dropped in about nine o'clock to ask her opinion as to the hymns on Sunday; and finding Miss Trix and Newhaven in the small drawing-room, he sat down and talked to them. This was too much for Trix; she had treated him very kindly, and had allowed him to amuse her; but it was impossible to put up with presumption of that kind. Difficult as it was to discourage Mr. Ives, she did it, and he went away with a disconsolate puzzled expression. At the last moment, however, Trix so far relented as to express a hope that he was coming to tennis to-morrow, at which he brightened up a little. I do not wish to be uncharitable—least of all to a charming young lady—but my opinion is that Miss Trix did not wish to set the curate altogether adrift. I think, however, that Lady Queenborough must have spoken again; for when Jack did come to tennis, Trix treated him with the most freezing civility and a hardly disguised disdain, and devoted herself to Lord Newhaven with as much assiduity as her mother could wish. We men, over our pipes, expressed the opinion that Jack Ives's little hour of sunshine was past, and that nothing was left to us but to look on at the prosperous uneventful course of Lord Newhaven's wooing. Trix had had her fun (so Algy Stanton bluntly phrased it) and would now settle down to business.

"I believe, though," he added, "that she likes the curate a bit, you know."

During the whole of the next day— Wednesday—Jack Ives kept away; he had, apparently, accepted the inevitable, and was healing his wounded heart by a strict attention to his parochial duties. Newhaven remarked on his absence with an air of relief; and Miss Trix treated it as a matter of no importance; Lady Queenborough was all smiles; and Dora Polton restricted herself to exclaiming, as I sat by her at tea, in a

low tone and *à propos* to nothing in particular,
" Oh, well,—poor Mr. Ives ! "

But on Thursday there occurred an event,
the significance of which passed at the moment
unperceived, but which had in fact most
important results. This was no other than
the arrival of little Mrs. Wentworth, an intimate friend of Dora's. Mrs. Wentworth had
been left a widow early in life ; she possessed
a comfortable competence ; she was not handsome, but she was vivacious, amusing, and,
above all, sympathetic. She sympathised at
once with Lady Queenborough in her maternal
anxieties, with Trix on her charming romance,
with Newhaven on his sweet devotedness,
with the rest of us on our obvious desolation
—and, after a confidential chat with Dora,
she sympathised most strongly with poor Mr.
Ives on his unfortunate attachment. Nothing
would satisfy her, so Dora told me, except
the opportunity of plying Mr. Ives with her
soothing balm ; and Dora was about to sit
down and write him a note, when he strolled
in through the drawing-room window, and
announced that his cook's mother was ill,
and that he should be very much obliged if
Mrs. Polton would give him some dinner that
evening. Trix and Newhaven happened to

enter by the door at the same moment, and Jack darted up to them, and shook hands with the greatest effusion. He had evidently buried all unkindness—and with it, we hoped, his mistaken folly. However that might be, he made no effort to engross Trix, but took his seat most docilely by his hostess; and she, of course, introduced him to Mrs. Wentworth. His behaviour was, in fact, so exemplary, that even Lady Queenborough relaxed her severity, and condescended to cross-examine him on the morals and manners of the old women of the parish. " Oh, the Vicar looks after them," said Jack; and he turned to Mrs. Wentworth again.

There can be no doubt that Mrs. Wentworth had a remarkable power of sympathy. I took her in to dinner, and she was deep in the subject of my " noble and inspiring art," before the soup was off the table. Indeed I'm sure that my life's ambitions would have been an open book to her by the time that the joint arrived, had not Jack Ives, who was sitting on the lady's other side, cut into the conversation just as Mrs. Wentworth was comparing my early struggles with those of Mr. Carlyle. After this intervention of Jack's I had not a chance. I ate my dinner without

the sauce of sympathy, substituting for it
a certain amusement which I derived from
studying the face of Miss Trix Queenborough,
who was placed on the opposite side of the
table. And if Trix did look now and again at
Mrs. Wentworth and Jack Ives, I cannot say
that her conduct was unnatural. To tell the
truth, Jack was so obviously delighted with
his new friend that it was quite pleasant—
and, as I say, under the circumstances,
rather amusing—to watch them. We felt
that the Squire was justified in having a hit
at Jack when Jack said, in the smoking-
room, that he found himself rather at a loss
for a subject for his next sermon.

"What do you say," suggested my cousin,
puffing at his pipe, " to taking constancy as
your text ?"

Jack considered the idea for a moment, but
then he shook his head.

"No. I think," he said reflectively,
"that I shall preach on the power of
sympathy."

That sermon afforded me—I must confess
it, at the risk of seeming frivolous—very
great entertainment. Again I secured a
place by Miss Trix—on her left, Newhaven
being on her right; and her face was worth

study when Jack Ives gave us a most eloquent description of the wonderful gift in question. It was, he said, the essence and the crown of true womanliness, and it showed itself—well, to put it quite plainly, it showed itself, according to Jack Ives, in exactly that sort of manner and bearing which so honourably and gracefully distinguished Mrs. Wentworth. The lady was not, of course, named, but she was clearly indicated. "Your gift, your precious gift," cried the Curate, apostrophising the impersonation of sympathy, "is given to you, not for your profit, but for mine. It is yours, but it is a trust to be used for me. It is yours, in fact, to share with me." At this climax, which must have struck upon her ear with a certain familiarity, Miss Trix Queenborough, notwithstanding the place and occasion, tossed her pretty head and whispered to me, "What horrid stuff!"

In the ensuing week Jack Ives was our constant companion; the continued illness of his servant's mother left him stranded, and Dora's kind heart at once offered him the hospitality of her roof. For my part I was glad, for the little drama which now began was not without its interest. It was a pleasant change to see Jack genially polite to Trix Queenborough, but quite indifferent to her presence or absence, and content to allow her to take Newhaven for her partner at tennis as often as she pleased. He himself was often an absentee from our games. Mrs. Wentworth did not play, and Jack would sit under the trees with her, or take her out in the canoe. What Trix thought I did not know, but it is a fact that she treated poor Newhaven like dirt beneath her feet, and that Lady Queenborough's face began to lose its transiently pleasant expression. I had a vague idea that a retribution was working itself out, and disposed myself to see the process with all the complacency induced by the spectacle of others receiving punishment for their sins.

A little scene which occurred after lunch one day was significant. I was sitting on the terrace, ready booted and breeched, waiting for my horse to be brought round. Trix came out and sat down by me.

" Where's Newhaven ? " I asked.

" Oh, I don't always want Lord Newhaven," she exclaimed petulantly ; " I sent him off for a walk. I'm going out in the Canadian canoe with Mr. Ives."

"Oh, you are, are you?" said I, smiling.

As I spoke, Jack Ives ran up to us.

"I say, Miss Queenborough," he cried, "I've just got your message saying you'd let me take you on the lake."

"Is it a great bore?" asked Trix, with a glance—a glance that meant mischief.

"I should like it awfully, of course," said Jack; "but the fact is I've promised to take Mrs. Wentworth—before I got your message, you know."

Trix drew herself up.

"Of course, if Mrs. Wentworth—— " she began.

"I'm very sorry," said Jack.

Then Miss Queenborough, forgetting—as I hope—or choosing to disregard my presence, leant forward and asked in her most coaxing tones,

"Don't you ever forget a promise, Mr. Ives?"

Jack looked at her. I suppose her dainty prettiness struck him afresh, for he wavered and hesitated.

"She's gone upstairs," pursued the tempter, "and we shall be safe away before she comes down again."

Jack shuffled with one foot on the gravel.

" I tell you what," he said. " I'll ask her if she minds me taking you for a little while before I——"

I believe he really thought that he had hit upon a compromise satisfactory to all parties. If so, he was speedily undeceived. Trix flushed red and answered angrily,

" Pray don't trouble. I don't want to go."

" Perhaps afterwards you might——" suggested the Curate, but now rather timidly.

" I'm going out with Lord Newhaven," said she. And she added in an access of uncontrollable annoyance, " Go, please go. I don't want you."

Jack sheered off, with a look of puzzled shamefacedness. He disappeared into the house. Nothing passed between Miss Trix and myself. A moment later Newhaven came out.

" Why, Miss Queenborough," said he, in apparent surprise, " Ives is going with Mrs. Wentworth in the canoe ! "

In an instant I saw what she had done. In rash presumption she had told Newhaven that she was going with the Curate ; and now the Curate had refused to take her ; and Newhaven had met him in search of Mrs. Wentworth. What could she do ? Well, she rose—or fell—to the occasion. In the coldest of voices she said,

"I thought you'd gone for your walk."

"I was just starting," he answered apologetically, "when I met Ives. But, as you weren't going with him——" He paused, an inquiring look in his eyes. He was evidently asking himself why she had not gone with the Curate.

"I'd rather be left alone, if you don't mind," said she. And then, flushing red again, she added, "I changed my mind and refused to go with Mr. Ives. So he went off to get Mrs. Wentworth instead."

I started. Newhaven looked at her for an instant, and then turned on his heel. She turned to me, quick as lightning, and with her face all aflame,

"If you tell, I'll never speak to you again," she whispered.

After this there was a silence for some minutes.

"Well?" she said, without looking at me.

"I have no remark to offer, Miss Queenborough," I returned.

"I suppose that was a lie, wasn't it?" she asked defiantly.

"It's not my business to say what it was," was my discreet answer.

"I know what you're thinking."

"I was thinking," said I, "which I would rather be—the man you will marry, or the man you would like—— "

"How dare you? It's not true. Oh, Mr. Wynne, indeed it's not true!"

Whether it were true or not I did not know. But if it had been, Miss Trix Queenborough might have been expected to act very much in the way in which she proceeded to act: that is to say, to be extravagantly attentive to Lord Newhaven when Jack Ives was present, and markedly neglectful of him in the Curate's absence. It also fitted in very well with the theory which I had ventured to hint, that her bearing towards Mrs. Wentworth was distinguished by a stately civility, and her remarks about that lady by a superfluity of laudation; for if these be not two distinguishing marks of rivalry in the well-bred, I must go back to my favourite books and learn from them—more folly. And if Trix's manners were all that they should be, praise no less high must be accorded to Mrs. Wentworth's; she attained an altitude of admirable unconsciousness, and conducted her flirtation (the poverty of language forces me to the word, but it is over-flippant) with the Curate in a staid, quasi-maternal way. She called him a delightful boy, and said that she was intensely interested in all his aims and hopes.

"What does she want?" I asked Dora despairingly. "She can't want to marry him." I was referring to Trix Queenborough, not to Mrs. Wentworth.

"Good gracious, no!" answered Dora irritably. "It's simple jealousy. She won't let the poor boy alone till he's in love with her again. It's a horrible shame!"

"Oh, well, he has great recuperative power," said I.

"She'd better be careful, though. It's a very dangerous game. How do you suppose Lord Newhaven likes it?"

Accident gave me that very day a hint how little Lord Newhaven liked it, and a glimpse of the risk Miss Trix was running. Entering the library suddenly, I heard Newhaven's voice raised above his ordinary tones.

"I won't stand it," he was declaring. "I never know how she'll treat me from one minute to the next."

My entrance, of course, stopped the

conversation very abruptly. Newhaven had come to a stand in the middle of the room, and Lady Queenborough sat on the sofa, a formidable frown on her brow. Withdrawing myself as rapidly as possible, I argued the probability of a severe lecture for Miss Trix, ending in a command to try her noble suitor's patience no longer. I hope all this happened, for I, not seeing why Mrs. Wentworth should monopolise the grace of sympathy, took the liberty of extending mine to Newhaven. He was certainly in love with Trix, not with her money, and the treatment he underwent must have been as trying to his feelings as it was galling to his pride.

My sympathy was not premature, for Miss Trix's fascinations, which were indubitably great, began to have their effect. The scene about the canoe was re-enacted, but with a different *dénoûment.* This time the promise was forgotten, and the widow forsaken. Then Mrs. Wentworth put on her armour. We had, in fact, reached this very absurd situation, that these two ladies were contending for the favours of, or the domination over, such an obscure, poverty-stricken, hopelessly ineligible person as the Curate of Poltons undoubtedly was. The position seemed to me then, and still seems, to indicate some re-markable qualities in that young man.

At last Newhaven made a move. At break-fast, on Wednesday morning, he announced that, reluctant as he should be to leave Poltons Park, he was due at his aunt's place, in Kent, on Saturday evening, and must therefore make his arrangements to leave by noon on that day. The significance was ap-parent. Had he come down to breakfast with "Now or Never!" stamped in fiery letters across his brow, it would have been more obtrusive indeed, but not a whit plainer. We all looked down at our plates, except Jack Ives. He flung one glance (I saw it out of the corner of my left eye) at Newhaven, another at Trix; then he remarked kindly,

"We shall be uncommonly sorry to lose you, Newhaven."

Events began to happen now, and I will tell them as well as I am able, supplementing my own knowledge by what I learnt after-wards from Dora—she having learnt it from the actors in the scene. In spite of the solemn warning conveyed in Newhaven's inti-mation, Trix, greatly daring, went off imme-diately after lunch for what she described as " a long ramble " with Mr. Ives. There was, indeed, the excuse of an old woman at the end of the ramble, and Trix provided Jack with a small basket of comforts for the useful old body; but the ramble was, we felt, the thing, and I was much annoyed at not being able to accompany the walkers in the cloak of darkness or other invisible contrivance. The ramble consumed three hours — full measure. Indeed, it was half-past six before Trix, alone, walked up the drive. Newhaven, a solitary figure, paced up and down the terrace fronting the drive. Trix came on, her head thrown back and a steady smile on her lips. She saw Newhaven : he stood looking at her for a moment with what she afterwards described as an indescribable smile on his face, but not, as Dora understood from her, by any means a pleasant one. Yet, if not pleasant, there is not the least doubt in the world that it was highly significant; for she cried out nervously,

"Why are you looking at me like that? What's the matter?"

Newhaven, still saying nothing, turned his back on her and made as if he would walk into the house and leave her there, ignored, discarded, done with. She, realising the crisis which had come, forgetting everything except the imminent danger of losing him once for all, without time for long explanation or any roundabout seductions, ran forward, laying her hand on his arm, and blurting out,

"But I've refused him."

I do not know what Newhaven thinks now, but I sometimes doubt whether he would not have been wiser to shake off the detaining hand and pursue his lonely way, first into the house, and ultimately to his aunt's. But (to say nothing of the twenty thousand a year, which, after all, and be you as romantic as you may please to be, is not a thing to be sneezed at) Trix's face, its mingled eagerness and shame, its flushed cheeks and shining eyes, the piquancy of its unwonted humility, overcame him. He stopped dead.

"I—I was obliged to give him an—an opportunity," said Miss Trix, having the grace to stumble a little in her speech. "And—and it's all your fault."

The war was thus, by happy audacity, carried into Newhaven's own quarters.

"My fault!" he exclaimed. "My fault that you walk all day with that curate!"

Then Miss Trix—and let no irrelevant considerations mar the appreciation of fine acting —dropped her eyes and murmured softly,

"I—I was so terribly afraid of seeming to expect *you*."

Wherewith she (and not he) ran away, lightly, up the stairs, turning just one glance downwards as she reached the landing. Newhaven was looking up from below with an "enchanted" smile—the word is Trix's own : I should probably have used a different one.

Was then the Curate of Poltons utterly defeated—brought to his knees, only to be spurned ? It seemed so : and he came down to dinner that night with a subdued and melancholy expression. Trix, on the other hand, was brilliant and talkative to the last degree, and the gaiety spread from her all round the table, leaving untouched only the rejected lover and Mrs. Wentworth; for the last-named lady, true to her distinguishing quality, had begun to talk to poor Jack Ives in low soothing tones.

After dinner Trix was not visible; but the door of the little boudoir beyond stood half open, and very soon Newhaven edged his way through. Almost at the same moment Jack Ives and Mrs. Wentworth passed out of the window and began to walk up and down the gravel. Nobody but myself appeared to notice these remarkable occurrences, but

I watched them with keen interest. Half an hour passed, and then there smote on my watchful ear the sound of a low laugh from the boudoir. It was followed almost immediately by a stranger sound from the gravel walk. Then, all in a moment, two things happened. The boudoir door opened, and Trix, followed by Newhaven, came in smiling; from the window entered Jack Ives and Mrs. Wentworth. My eyes were on the Curate. He gave one sudden comprehending glance towards the other couple; then he took the widow's hand, led her up to Dora, and said, in low yet penetrating tones,

"Will you wish us joy, Mrs. Polton?"

The Squire, Rippleby, and Algy Stanton were round them in an instant. I kept my place, watching now the face of Trix Queenborough. She turned first flaming red, then very pale. I saw her turn to Newhaven and speak one or two urgent imperative words to him. Then, drawing herself up to her full height, she crossed the room to where the group was assembled round Mrs. Wentworth and Jack Ives.

"What's the matter? What are you saying?" she asked.

Mrs. Wentworth's eyes were modestly cast

down, but a smile played round her mouth. No one spoke for a moment. Then Jack Ives said,

"Mrs. Wentworth has promised to be my wife, Miss Queenborough."

For a moment, hardly perceptible, Trix hesitated; then, with the most winning, touching, sweetest smile in the world, she said,

"So you took my advice, and our afternoon walk was not wasted after all!"

Mrs. Polton is not used to these fine flights of diplomacy; she had heard before dinner something (not all) of what had actually happened in the afternoon; and the simple woman positively jumped. Jack Ives met Trix's scornful eyes full and square.

"Not at all wasted," said he, with a smile. "Not only has it shown me where my true happiness lies, but it has also given me a juster idea of the value and sincerity of your regard for me, Miss Queenborough."

"It is as real, Mr. Ives, as it is sincere," said she.

"It is like yourself, Miss Queenborough," said he, with a low bow; and he turned from her and began to talk to his *fiancée*.

Trix Queenborough moved slowly towards

where I sat. Newhaven was watching her from where he stood alone on the other side of the room.

"And have you no news for us?" I asked in low tones.

"Thank you," she said haughtily; "I don't care that mine should be a pendant to the great tidings about the little widow and the Curate."

After a moment's pause she went on:

"He lost no time, did he? He was wise to secure her before what happened this afternoon could leak out. Nobody can tell her now."

"This afternoon?"

"He asked me to marry him this afternoon."

"And you refused?"

"Yes."

"Well, his behaviour is in outrageously bad taste, but—— "

She laid a hand on my arm, and said in calm level tones,

"I refused him because I dared not have him; but I told him I cared for him, and he said he loved me. And I let him kiss me. Good-night, Mr. Wynne."

I sat still and silent. Newhaven came

across to us. Trix put out her hand and caught him by the sleeve.

"Fred," she said, "my dear honest old Fred, you love me, don't you?"

Newhaven, much embarrassed and surprised, looked at me in alarm. But her hand was in his now, and her eyes implored him.

"I should rather think I did, my dear," said he.

I really hope that Lord and Lady Newhaven will not be very unhappy, while Mrs. Ives quite worships her husband, and is convinced that she eclipsed the brilliant and wealthy Miss Queenborough. Perhaps she did — perhaps not. There are, as I have said, great qualities in the Curate of Poltons, but I have not quite made up my mind precisely what they are. I ought, however, to say that Dora takes a more favourable view of him and a less lenient view of Trix than I. That is perhaps natural. Besides, Dora does not know the precise manner in which the Curate was refused. By the way, he preached next Sunday on the text, "The children of this world are wiser in their generation than the children of light."

A THREE-VOLUME NOVEL.

It was, I believe, mainly as a compliment to me that Miss Audrey Liston was asked to Poltons. Miss Liston and I were very good friends, and my cousin Dora Polton thought, as she informed me, that it would be nice for me to have some one I could talk to about "books, and so on." I did not complain. Miss Liston was a pleasant young woman of six and twenty; I liked her very much except on paper, and I was aware that she made it a point of duty to read something at least of what I wrote. She was in the habit of describing herself as an "authoress in a small way." If it were pointed out that six three-volume novels in three years (the term of her literary activity, at the time of which I write) could hardly be called "a small way," she would smile modestly and say that it was not really much; and if she were told that the

English language embraced no such word as "authoress," she would smile again and say that it ought to—a position towards the bugbear of correctness with which, I confess, I sympathise in some degree. She was very diligent; she worked from ten to one every day while she was at Poltons; how much she wrote is between her and her conscience.

There was another impeachment which Miss Liston was hardly at the trouble to deny. "Take my characters from life?" she would exclaim. "Surely every artist" (Miss Liston often referred to herself as an artist) "must?" And she would proceed to maintain—what is perhaps true sometimes—that people rather liked being put into books, just as they like being photographed, for all that they grumble and pretend to be afflicted when either process is levied against them. In discussing this matter with Miss Liston, I felt myself on delicate ground, for it was notorious that I figured in her first book in the guise of a misogynistic genius. The fact that she lengthened (and thickened) my hair, converted it from an indeterminate brown to a dusky black, gave me a drooping moustache, and invested my very ordinary work-a-day eyes with a strange magnetic attraction, availed nothing; I was at once recognised, and, I may remark in passing, an uncommonly disagreeable fellow she made me. Thus I had passed through the fire. I felt tolerably sure that I presented no other aspect of interest, real or supposed, and I was quite content that Miss Liston should serve all the rest of her acquaintance as she had served me. I reckoned they would last her, at the present rate of production, about five years.

Fate was kind to Miss Liston, and provided her with most suitable patterns for her next piece of work at Poltons itself. There were a young man and a young woman staying in the house—Sir Gilbert Chillington and Miss Pamela Myles. The moment Miss Liston was apprised of a possible romance, she began the study of the protagonists. She was looking out, she told me, for some new types (if it were any consolation—and there is a sort of dignity about it—to be called a type, Miss Liston's victims were always welcome to so much), and she had found them in Chillington and Pamela. The former appeared to my dull eye to offer no salient novelty; he was tall, broad, handsome, and he possessed a manner of enviable placidity. Pamela, I allowed, was exactly the heroine Miss Liston loved—

haughty, capricious, *difficile*, but sound and true at heart. (I was mentally skimming Volume I.) Miss Liston agreed with me in my conception of Pamela, but declared that I did not do justice to the artistic possibilities latent in Chillington; he had a curious attraction which it would tax her skill (so she gravely informed me) to the utmost to reproduce. She proposed that I also should make a study of him, and attributed my hurried refusal to a shrinking from the difficulties of the task.

"Of course," she observed, looking at our young friends, who were talking nonsense at the other side of the lawn, "they must have a misunderstanding."

"Why, of course," said I, lighting my pipe. "What should you say to another man?"

"Or another woman?" said Miss Liston.

"It comes to the same thing," said I. (About a volume and a half, I meant.)

"But it's more interesting. Do you think she'd better be a married woman?" And Miss Liston looked at me inquiringly.

"The age prefers them married," I remarked.

This conversation happened on the second day of Miss Liston's visit, and she lost no

time in beginning to study her subjects.
Pamela, she said, she found pretty plain sail-
ing, but Chillington continued to puzzle her.
Again, she could not make up her mind
whether to have a happy or a tragic ending.
In the interests of a tender-hearted public, I
pleaded for marriage-bells.

"Yes, I think so," said Miss Liston, but
she sighed, and I think she had an idea or
two for a heart-broken separation, followed by
mutual, lifelong, hopeless devotion.

The complexity of young Sir Gilbert did
not, in Miss Liston's opinion, appear less on
further acquaintance; and indeed, I must
admit that she was not altogether wrong in
considering him worthy of attention. As I
came to know him better, I discerned in him
a smothered self-appreciation, which came to
light in response to the least tribute of interest
or admiration, but was yet far remote from the
aggressiveness of a commonplace vanity. In
a moment of indiscretion I had chaffed him—
he was very good-natured—on the risks he
ran at Miss Liston's hands. He was not disgusted, but neither did he plume himself or
spread his feathers. He received the suggestion without surprise and without any
attempt at disclaiming fitness for the purpose;

but he received it as a matter which entailed a responsibility on him. I detected the conviction that, if the portrait were to be painted, it was due to the world that it should be well painted; the subject must give the artist full opportunities.

"What does she know about me?" he asked in meditative tones.

"She's very quick; she'll soon pick up as much as she wants," I assured him.

"She'll probably go all wrong," he said sombrely; and of course I could not tell him that it was of no consequence if she did. He would not have believed me, and would have done precisely what he proceeded to do, and that was to afford Miss Liston every chance of appraising his character and plumbing the depths of his soul. I may say at once that I did not regret this course of action; for the effect of it was to allow me a chance of talking to Pamela Myles, and Pamela was exactly the sort of girl to beguile the long pleasant morning hours of a holiday in the country. No one had told Pamela that she was going to be put in a book, and I don't think it would have made any difference had she been told. Pamela's attitude towards books was one of healthy scorn, confidently based on admitted ignorance. So we never spoke of them, and my cousin Dora condoled with me more than once on the way in which Miss Liston, false to the implied terms of her invitation, deserted me in favour of Sir Gilbert, and left me to the mercies of a frivolous girl. Pamela appeared to be as little aggrieved as I was. I imagined that she supposed that Chillington would ask her to marry him some day before very long, and I was sure she would accept him ; but it was quite plain that, if Miss Liston persisted in making Pamela her heroine, she would have to supply from her own resources a large supplement of passion. Pamela was far too deficient in the commodity to be made anything of, without such reinforcement, even by an art more adept at making much out of nothing than Miss Liston's straightforward method could claim to be.

A week passed, and then, one Friday morning, a new light burst on me. Miss Liston came into the garden at eleven o'clock and sat down by me on the lawn. Chillington and Pamela had gone riding with the Squire, Dora was visiting the poor. We were alone. The appearance of Miss Liston at this hour (usually sacred to the use of the pen), no less than her puzzled look, told me that an obstruction had occurred in the novel. Presently she let me know what it was.

" I'm thinking of altering the scheme of my story, Mr. Wynne," said she. " Have you ever noticed how sometimes a man thinks he's in love when he isn't really ? "

" Such a case sometimes occurs," I acknowledged.

" Yes, and he doesn't find out his mistake—— "

" Till they're married ? "

" Sometimes, yes," she said, rather as though she were making an unwilling admission. " But sometimes he sees it before; when he meets somebody else."

" Very true," said I with a grave nod.

" The false can't stand against the real," pursued Miss Liston; and then she fell into meditative silence. I stole a glance at her face; she was smiling. Was it in the pleasure of literary creation—an artistic ecstacy? I should have liked to answer yes, but I doubted it very much. Without pretending to Miss Liston's powers, I have the little subtlety that is needful to show me that more than one kind of smile may be seen on the human face, and that there is one very different from others; and, finally, that that one is not evoked, as a rule, merely by the evolution of the troublesome encumbrance to pretty writing, vulgarly called a "plot."

"If," pursued Miss Liston, "some one comes who can appreciate him and draw out what is best in him——"

"That's all very well," said I; "but what of the first girl?"

"Oh, she's—she can be made shallow, you know; and I can put in a man for her. People needn't be much interested in her."

"Yes, you could manage it that way," said I, thinking how Pamela—I took the liberty of using her name for the shallow girl—would like such treatment.

"She will really be valuable mainly as a foil," observed Miss Liston; and she added generously, "I shall make her nice, you know, but shallow—not worthy of him."

"And what are you going to make the other girl like?" I asked.

Miss Liston started slightly; also she coloured very slightly, and she answered, looking away from me across the lawn,

"I haven't quite made up my mind yet, Mr. Wynne."

With the suspicion which this conversation aroused fresh in my mind, it was curious to hear Pamela laugh, as she said to me on the afternoon of the same day,

"Aren't Sir Gilbert and Audrey Liston funny? I tell you what, Mr. Wynne, I believe they're writing a novel together."

"Perhaps Chillington's giving her the materials for one," I suggested.

"I shouldn't think," observed Pamela in her dispassionate way, "that anything very interesting had ever happened to him."

"I thought you liked him," I remarked humbly.

"So I do. What's that got to do with it?" asked Pamela.

It was beyond question that Chillington enjoyed Miss Liston's society; the interest she showed in him was incense to his nostrils. I used to overhear fragments of his ideas about himself which he was revealing in answer to her tactful inquiries. But neither was it doubtful that he had by no means lost his relish for Pamela's lighter talk; in fact, he seemed to turn to her with some relief; perhaps it is refreshing to escape from self-analysis, even when the process is conducted in the pleasantest possible manner; and the hours which Miss Liston gave to work were devoted by Chillington to maintaining his cordial relations with the lady whose comfortable and not over-tragical disposal was taxing Miss Liston's skill. For she had definitely decided on her plot—she told me so a few days later. It was all planned out; nay, the scene in which the truth as to his own feelings bursts on Sir Gilbert (I forget at the moment what name the novel gave him) was, I understood, actually written; the shallow girl was to experience nothing worse than a wound to her vanity, and was to turn with as much alacrity as decency allowed to the substitute whom Miss Liston had now provided. All this was poured into my sympathetic ear, and I say sympathetic in all sincerity; for, although I may occasionally treat Miss Liston's literary efforts with less than proper respect, she herself was my friend, and the conviction under which she was now living would, I knew, unless it were justified, bring her into much of that unhappiness in which one generally found her heroine plunged about the end of Volume II. The heroine generally got out all right, and the knowledge that she would enabled the reader to preserve cheerfulness. But would poor little Miss Liston get out? I was none too sure of it.

Suddenly a change came in the state of affairs. Pamela produced it. It must have struck her that the increasing intimacy of Miss Liston and Chillington might become something other than "funny." To put it briefly and metaphorically, she whistled her dog back to her heels. I am not skilled in understanding or describing the artifices of ladies; but even I saw the transformation in Pamela. She put forth her strength and put on her prettiest gowns; she refused to take her place in the seesaw of society, which Chillington had recently established for his pleasure. If he spent an hour with Miss Liston, Pamela would have nothing of him for a day; she met his attentions with scorn unless they were undivided. Chillington seemed at first puzzled—I believe that he never regarded his talks with Miss Liston in other than a business point of view—but directly he understood that Pamela claimed him, and that she was prepared, in case he did not obey her call, to establish a grievance against him, he lost no time in manifesting his obedience. A whole day passed in which, to my certain knowledge, he was not alone a moment with Miss Liston, and did not, save at the family meals, exchange a word with her. As he walked off with Pamela, Miss Liston's eyes followed him in wistful longing; she stole away upstairs, and did not come down till five o'clock. Then, finding me strolling about with a cigarette, she joined me.

" Well, how goes the book ? " I asked.

" I haven't done much to it just lately," she answered in a low voice. " I—it's—I don't quite know what to do with it."

" I thought you'd settled ? "

" So I had, but——Oh, don't let's talk about it, Mr. Wynne ! "

But a moment later she went on talking about it.

" I don't know why I should make it end happily," she said. " I'm sure life isn't always happy, is it ? "

" Certainly not," I answered. " You mean your man might stick to the shallow girl, after all ? "

" Yes," I just heard her whisper.

" And be miserable afterwards ? " I pursued.

" I don't know," said Miss Liston. " Perhaps he wouldn't."

" Then you must make him shallow himself."

" I can't do that," she said quickly. " Oh, how difficult it is ! "

She may have meant merely the art of writing—when I cordially agree with her—but I think she meant also the way of the world, which does not make me withdraw my assent. I left her walking up and down in front of the drawing-room windows—a rather forlorn little figure, thrown into distinctness by the cold rays of the setting sun.

All was not over yet. That evening Chillington broke away. Led by vanity, or interest, or friendliness, I know not which—tired maybe of paying court (the attitude in which Pamela kept him), and thinking it would be pleasant to play the other part for a while—after dinner he went straight to Miss Liston, talked to her while we had coffee on the terrace, and then walked about with her. Pamela sat by me; she was very silent; she did not appear to be angry, but her handsome mouth wore a resolute expression. Chillington and Miss Liston wandered on into the shrubbery, and did not come into sight again for nearly half an hour.

"I think it's cold," said Pamela in her cool quiet tones. "And it's also, Mr. Wynne, rather slow. I shall go to bed."

I thought it a little impertinent of Pamela

to attribute the " slowness " (which had undoubtedly existed) to me, so I took my revenge by saying, with an assumption of innocence purposely and obviously unreal,

" Oh, but won't you wait and bid Miss Liston and Chillington good-night ? "

Pamela looked at me for a moment. I made bold to smile.

Pamela's face broke slowly into an answering smile.

" I don't know what you mean, Mr. Wynne," said she.

" No ? " said I.

" No," said Pamela, and she turned away. But before she went she looked over her shoulder, and, still smiling, said, " Wish Miss Liston good night for me, Mr. Wynne. Anything I have to say to Sir Gilbert will wait very well till to-morrow."

She had hardly gone in when the wanderers came out of the shrubbery and rejoined me. Chillington wore his usual passive look, but Miss Liston's face was happy and radiant. Chillington passed on into the drawing-room. Miss Liston lingered a moment by me.

" Why, you look," said I, " as if you'd invented the finest scene ever written."

She did not answer me directly, but stood

looking up at the stars. Then she said in a dreamy tone,

"I think I shall stick to my old idea in the book."

As she spoke, Chillington came out. Even in the dim light I saw a frown on his face.

"I say, Wynne," said he, "where's Miss Myles?"

"She's gone to bed," I answered. "She told me to wish you good night for her, Miss Liston. No message for you, Chillington."

Miss Liston's eyes were on him. He took no notice of her; he stood frowning for an instant, then, with some muttered ejaculation, he strode back into the house. We heard his heavy tread across the drawing-room; we heard the door slammed behind him, and I found myself looking on Miss Liston's altered face.

"What does he want her for, I wonder!" she said, in an agitation that made my presence, my thoughts, my suspicions, nothing to her. "He said nothing to me about wanting to speak to her to-night." And she walked slowly into the house, her eyes on the ground, and all the light gone from her face, and the joy dead in it. Whereupon I, left alone, began to rail at the gods that a dear silly little soul like Miss Liston should bother her poor silly little head about a hulking fool; in which reflections I did, of course, immense injustice not only to an eminent author, but also to a perfectly honourable, though somewhat dense and decidedly conceited, gentleman.

The next morning Sir Gilbert Chillington ate dirt—there is no other way of expressing it — in great quantities, and with infinite humility. My admirable friend Miss Pamela was severe. I saw him walk six yards behind her for the length of the terrace : not a look nor a turn of her head gave him leave to join her. Miss Liston had gone upstairs, and I watched the scene from the window of the smoking-room. At last, at the end of the long walk, just where the laurel-bushes mark the beginning of the shrubberies — on the threshold of the scene of his crime—Pamela turned round suddenly and faced the repentant sinner. The most interesting things in life are those which, perhaps by the inevitable nature of the case, one does not hear; and I did not hear the scene which followed. For a while they stood talking—rather, he talked and she listened. Then she turned again and walked slowly into the shrubbery.

Chillington followed. It was the end of a chapter, and I laid down the book.

How and from whom Miss Liston heard the news which Chillington himself told me without a glimmer of shame or a touch of embarrassment some two hours later, I do not know; but hear it she did before luncheon; for she came down, ready armed with the neatest little speeches for both the happy lovers. I did not expect Pamela to show an ounce more feeling than the strictest canons of propriety demanded, and she fulfilled my expectations to the letter; but I had hoped, I confess, that Chillington would have displayed some little consciousness. He did not; and it is my belief that, throughout the events which I have recorded, he retained, and that he still retains, the conviction that Miss Liston's interest in him was purely literary and artistic, and that she devoted herself to his society simply because he offered an interesting problem and an inspiring theme. An ingenious charity may find in that attitude evidence of modesty; to my thinking, it argues a more subtle and magnificent conceit than if he had fathomed the truth, as many humbler men in his place would have done.

On the day after the engagement was accomplished Miss Liston left us to return to London. She came out in her hat and jacket, and sat down by me; the carriage was to be round in ten minutes. She put on her gloves slowly, and buttoned them carefully. This done, she said,

"By the way, Mr. Wynne, I've adopted your suggestion. The man doesn't find out."

"Then you've made him a fool?" I asked bluntly.

"No," she answered. "I—I think it might happen though he wasn't a fool."

She sat with her hands in her lap for a moment or two, then she went on in a lower voice:

"I'm going to make him find out afterwards."

I felt her glance on me, but I looked straight in front of me.

"What, after he's married the shallow girl?"

"Yes," said Miss Liston.

"Rather too late, isn't it?—at least, if you mean there is to be a happy ending."

Miss Liston enlaced her fingers.

"I haven't decided about the ending yet," said she.

"If you're content to be tragical—which is the fashion—you'll do as you stand," said I.

"Yes," she answered slowly, "if I'm tragical, I shall do as I stand."

There was another pause, and rather a long one; the wheels of the carriage were audible on the gravel of the front drive. Miss Liston stood up. I rose and held out my hand.

"Of course," said Miss Liston, still intent on her novel, "I could——" She stopped again, and looked apprehensively at me. My face, I believe, expressed nothing more than polite attention and friendly interest.

"Of course," she began again, " the shallow girl — his wife — might — might die, Mr. Wynne."

"In novels," said I, with a smile, " while there's death, there's hope."

"Yes, in novels," she answered, giving me her hand.

The poor little woman was very unhappy. Unwisely, I dare say, I pressed her hand. It was enough; the tears leapt to her eyes; she gave my great fist a hurried squeeze—I have seldom been more touched by any thanks, however warm or eloquent—and hurried away.

I have read the novel. It came out a little while ago. The man finds out after the marriage; the shallow girl dies unregretted (she turns out as badly as possible); the real love comes, and all ends joyfully. It is a simple story prettily told in its little way, and the scene of the reunion is written with genuine feeling—nay, with a touch of real passion. But then Sir Gilbert Chillington never meets Miss Liston now. And Lady Chillington not only behaves with her customary propriety, but is in the enjoyment of most excellent health and spirits.

True art demands an adaptation, not a copy, of life. I saw that remark somewhere the other day. It seems correct, if Miss Liston be any authority.

THE DECREE OF DUKE DEODONATO.

"It is a most anxious thing to be an absolute ruler," said Duke Deodonato, "but I have made up my mind. The Doctor has convinced me"—here Dr. Fusbius, Ph.D., bowed very low—"that marriage is the best, noblest, wholesomest, and happiest of human conditions."

"Your Highness will remember——" began the President of the Council.

"My Lord, I have made up my mind," said Duke Deodonato.

Thus speaking, the Duke took a large sheet of foolscap paper, and wrote rapidly for a moment or two.

"There," he said, pushing the paper over to the President, "is the decree."

"The decree, sir?"

"I think three weeks afford ample space," said Duke Deodonato.

" Three weeks, sir ? "

" For every man over twenty-one years of age in this Duchy to find himself a wife."

" Your Highness," observed Dr. Fusbius with deference, " will consider that between an abstract proposition and a practical measure——"

" There is to the logical mind no stopping-place," interrupted Duke Deodonato.

" But, sir," cried the President, " imagine the consternation which this——!"

" Let it be gazetted to-night," said Duke Deodonato.

" I would venture," said the President, " to remind Your Highness that you are yourself a bachelor."

" Laws," said Duke Deodonato, " do not bind the Crown unless the Crown is expressly mentioned."

" True, sir; but I humbly conceive that it would be *pessimi exempli*——"

" You are right; I will marry myself," said Duke Deodonato.

" But, sir, three weeks ! The hand of a Princess cannot be requested and granted in——"

" Then find me somebody else," said Deodonato ; " and pray leave me. I would be alone;" and Duke Deodonato waved his hand to the door.

Outside the door, the President said to the Doctor,

"I could wish, sir, that you had not convinced His Highness."

"My lord," rejoined the Doctor, "truth is my only preoccupation."

"Sir," said the President, "are you married?"

"My Lord," answered the Doctor, "I am not."

"I thought not," said the President, as he folded up the decree and put it in his pocket.

It is useless to deny that Duke Deodonato's decree caused considerable disturbance in the Duchy. In the first place, the Crown lawyers raised a puzzle of law. Did the word "man," as used in the decree, include "woman"? The President shook his head, and referred the question to His Highness.

"It seems immaterial," observed the Duke. "If a man marries, a woman marries."

"*Ex vi terminorum,*" assented the Doctor.

"But, sir," said the President, "there are more women than men in the Duchy."

Duke Deodonato threw down his pen.

"This is very provoking," said he. "Why was it allowed? I'm sure it happened before *I* came to the throne."

The Doctor was about to point out that it could hardly have been guarded against, when the President (who was a better courtier) anticipated him.

"We did not foresee that Your Highness, in Your Highness's wisdom, would issue this decree," he said humbly.

"True," said Duke Deodonato, who was a just man.

"Would Your Highness vouchsafe any explanation—— ?"

"What are the Judges for?" asked Duke Deodonato. "There is the law—let them interpret it."

Whereupon the Judges held that a "man" was not a "woman," and that although every man must marry, no woman need.

"It will make no difference," said the President.

"None at all," said Dr. Fusbius.

Nor, perhaps, would it, seeing that women are ever kind, and in no way by nature averse from marriage, had it not become known that Duke Deodonato himself intended to choose a wife from the ladies of his own dominions, and to choose her (according to the advice of Dr. Fusbius, who, in truth, saw little whither his counsel would in the end carry the Duke) without regard to such adventitious matters as rank or wealth, and purely for her beauty, talent, and virtue. Which resolve being proclaimed, straightway all the ladies of the Duchy, of whatsoever station, calling, age, appearance, wit, or character, conceiving each of them that she, and no other, should become the Duchess, sturdily refused all offers of marriage (although they were many of them as desperately enamoured as virtuous ladies may be), and did nought else than walk, drive, ride, and display their charms in the park before the windows of the ducal palace. And thus it fell out that when a week had gone by, no man had obeyed Duke Deodonato's decree, and they were, from sheer want of brides, like to fall into contempt of the law and under the high displeasure of the Duke.

Upon this the President and Dr. Fusbius sought audience of His Highness, and humbly laid before him the unforeseen obstacle which had occurred.

"Woman is ever ambitious," said Dr. Fusbius.

"Nay," corrected the President, "they have seen His Highness's person as His Highness has ridden through the city."

Duke Deodonato threw down his pen.

"This is very tiresome," said he, knitting his brows. "My Lord, I would be further advised on this matter. Return at the same hour to-morrow."

The next day, Duke Deodonato's forehead had regained its customary smoothness, and his manner was tranquil and assured.

"Our pleasure is," said he to the President, "that, albeit no woman shall be compelled to marry if so be that she be not invited thereunto; yet, if bidden, she shall in no wise refuse, but straightway espouse that man who first after the date of these presents shall solicit her hand."

The President bowed in admiration.

"It is, if I may humbly say so, a practical and wise solution, sir," he said.

"I apprehend that it will remedy the mischief," said Duke Deodonato, not ill-pleased.

And doubtless it would have had an effect as altogether satisfactory, excellent, beneficial, salutary, and universal as the wisdom of Duke Deodonato had anticipated from it, had it not fallen out that, on the promulgation of the decree, all the aforesaid ladies of the Duchy, of whatsoever station, calling, age, appearance, wit, or character, straightway, and so swiftly that no man had time wherein to pay his court to them, fled to and shut and bottled and barricaded themselves in houses, castles, cupboards, cellars, stables, lofts, churches, chapels, chests, and every other kind of receptacle whatsoever, and there remained beyond reach of any man, be he whom he would, lest haply one, coming, should ask their hand in marriage, and thus they should lose all prospect of wedding the Duke.

When Duke Deodonato was apprised of this lamentable action on the part of the ladies of the Duchy, he frowned and laid down his pen.

" This is very annoying," said he. " There appears to be a disposition to thwart Our endeavours for the public good."

" It is gross contumacy," said Dr. Fusbius.

" Yet," remarked the President, " inspired by a natural, if ill-disciplined, admiration for His Highness's person."

" The decree is now a fortnight old," observed Duke Deodonato. " Leave me, I will consider further of this matter."

Now even as His Highness spoke a mighty

uproar arose under the palace windows, and Duke Deodonato, looking out of the window (which, be it remembered, but for the guidance of Heaven he might not have done), beheld a maiden of wonderful charms struggling in the clutches of two halberdiers of the guard, who were haling her off to prison.

"Bring hither that damsel," said Deodonato.

Presently the damsel, still held by the soldiers, entered the room. Her robe was dishevelled and rent, her golden hair hung loose on her shoulders, and her eyes were full of tears.

"At whose suit is she arrested?" asked Deodonato.

"At the suit of the most learned Dr. Fusbius, may it please Your Highness."

"Sir," said Dr. Fusbius, "it is true. This lady, grossly contemning Your Highness's decree, has refused my hand in marriage."

"Is it true, damsel?" asked Duke Deodonato.

"Hear me, Your Highness!" answered she. "I left my dwelling but an instant, for we were in sore straits for—— "

"Bread?" asked Deodonato, a touch of sympathy in his voice.

"May it please Your Highness, no—pins wherewith to fasten our hair. And, as I ran to the merchant's, this aged man—— "

"I am but turned of fifty," interrupted Fusbius.

"And have not yet learnt silence?" asked Deodonato severely. "Damsel, proceed!"

"Caught me by my gown as I ran and—— "

"I proposed marriage to her," said Fusbius.

"Nay, if you proposed marriage, she shall marry you," said Deodonato. "By the crown of my fathers, she shall marry you. But what said he, damsel?"

"May it please Your Highness, he said that I had the prettiest face in all the Duchy, and that he would have no wife but me; and thereupon he kissed me; and I would have none of him, and I struck him and escaped."

"Send for the Judges," said Duke Deodonato. "And meanwhile keep this damsel, and let no man propose marriage to her until Our pleasure be known."

Now when the Judges were come, and the maiden was brought in and set over against them on the right hand, and the learned Doctor took his stand on the left, Deodonato prayed the Judges that they would perpend carefully and anxiously of the question—using all lore, research, wisdom, discretion, and justice—whether Dr. Fusbius had proposed marriage unto the maiden or no.

"Thus shalt Our mind be informed, and we shall deal profitably with this matter," concluded Duke Deodonato.

Upon which arose great debate. For there was one part of the learned men which leant upon the letter, and found no invitation to marriage in the words of Dr. Fusbius; while another part would have it that in all things the spirit and mind of the utterer must be regarded, and that it sorted not with the years, virtues, learning, and position of the said most learned Doctor to suppose that he had spoken such words, and sealed the same with a kiss, save under the firm impression, thought, and conviction that he was offering his hand in marriage; which said impression, thought, and conviction were fully and reasonably declared and evident in his actions, manner, bearing, air, and conduct.

"This is very perplexing," said Duke Deodonato, and he knit his brows; for as he gazed upon the beauty of the damsel, it seemed to him a thing unnatural, undesirable, unpalatable, unpleasant, and unendurable, that she should wed Dr. Fusbius. Yet if such were the law—Duke Deodonato sighed, and he glanced at the damsel: and it chanced that the damsel glanced at Duke Deodonato, and, seeing that he was a proper man and comely, and that his eye spoke his admiration of her, she blushed; and her cheek, that had gone white when those of the Judges who favoured the learned Doctor were speaking, went red as a rose again, and she strove to order her hair and to conceal the rent that was in her robe. And Duke Deodonato sighed again.

"My Lord," he said to the President, "we have heard these wise and erudite men; and, forasmuch as the matter is difficult, they are divided among themselves, and the staff whereon we leant is broken. Speak, therefore, your mind."

Then the President of the Council looked earnestly at Duke Deodonato, but the Duke veiled his face with his hand.

"Answer truly," said he, "without fear or favour; so shall you fulfil Our pleasure."

And the President, looking round upon the company, said:

"It is, Your Highness, by all reasonable,

honest, just, proper, and honourable intendment, as good, sound, full, and explicit an offer of marriage as hath ever been had in this Duchy."

"So be it," said Duke Deodonato; and Dr. Fusbius smiled in triumph, while the maiden grew pale again.

"And," pursued the President, "it binds, controls, and rules every man, woman, and child in these Your Highness's dominions, and hath the force of law over all."

"So be it," said Deodonato again.

"Saving," added the President, "Your Highness only."

There was a movement among the company.

"For," pursued the President, "by the ancient laws, customs, manners, and observances of the Duchy, no decree or law shall in any way whatsoever impair, alter, lessen, or derogate from the high rights, powers, and prerogatives of Your Highness, whom may Heaven long preserve. Although, therefore, it be, by and pursuant to Your Highness's decree, the sure right of every man in this Duchy to be accepted in marriage of any damsel whom he shall invite thereunto, yet is this right in all respects subject to and controlled by the natural, legal, inalienable, unalterable, and sovereign prerogative of Your Highness to marry what damsel soever it shall be Your pleasure to bid share your throne. Hence I, in obedience to your Highness's commands, pronounce and declare that this damsel is lawfully and irrevocably bound and affianced to the learned Dr. Fusbius, unless and until it shall please Your Highness yourself to demand her hand in marriage. May what I have spoken please Your Highness." And the President sat down.

Duke Deodonato sat awhile in thought, and there was silence in the Hall. Then he spoke:

"Let all withdraw, saving the damsel only."

And they one and all withdrew, and Duke Deodonato was left alone with the damsel.

Then he arose and gazed long on the damsel; but the damsel would not look on Duke Deodonato.

"How are you called, lady?" asked Duke Deodonato.

"I am called Dulcissima," said she.

"Well-named!" said Deodonato softly, and he went to the damsel, and he laid his hand, full gently, on her robe, and he said, "Dulcissima, you have the prettiest face in all the

Duchy, and I will have no wife but you;"
and Duke Deodonato kissed the damsel.

The damsel forbore to strike Duke Deodonato, as she had struck Dr. Fusbius. Again
her cheek went red, and again pale, and she
said,

"I wed no man on compulsion."

"Madam, I am Your Sovereign," said Duke
Deodonato ; and his eyes were on the damsel.

"If you were an Archangel——!" cried the
damsel.

"Our House is not wont to be scorned of
ladies," said Deodonato. "Am I crooked, or
baseborn, or a fool ? "

"This day in your Duchy women are slaves,
and men their masters by your will," said
she.

"It is the order of nature," said Deodonato.

"It is not my pleasure," said the damsel.

Then Deodonato laid his hand on his silver
bell, for he was very angry.

"Fusbius waits without," said he.

"I will wed him and kill him," cried
Dulcissima.

Deodonato gazed on her.

"You had no chance of using the pins,"
said he, "and the rent in your gown is very
sore."

Upon this the eyes of the damsel lost their fire and sought the floor; and she plucked at her girdle, and would not look on Deodonato. And they said outside,

"It is very still in the Hall of the Duke."

Then said Deodonato,

"Dulcissima, what would you?"

"That you repeal your decrees," said she.

Deodonato's brow grew dark; he did not love to go back.

"What I have decreed, I have decreed," said he.

"And what I have resolved, I have resolved," said she.

Deodonato drew near to her.

"And if I repeal the decrees?" said he.

"You will do well," said she.

"And you will wed—— ?"

"Whom I will," said she.

Deodonato turned to the window, and for a space he looked out. The damsel smoothed her hair and drew her robe, where it was whole, across the rent; and she looked on Deodonato as he stood, and her bosom rose and fell. And she prayed a prayer that no man heard or, if he heard, might be so base as to tell. But she saw the dark locks of Deodonato's hair and his form, straight as

an arrow and tall as a six-foot wand, in the
window. And again, outside, they said,

"It is strangely still in the Hall of the
Duke."

Then Deodonato turned, and he pressed
with his hand on the silver bell, and straightway the Hall was filled with the Councillors,
the Judges, and the halberdiers, attentive to
hear the will of Deodonato and the fate of
the damsel. And the small eyes of Fusbius
glowed, and the calm eyes of the President
smiled.

" My Cousins, Gentlemen, and my faithful
Guard," said Deodonato, " Time, which is
Heaven's mighty Instrument, brings counsel.
Say! What the Duke has done, shall any
man undo ? "

Then cried they all, save one,

" No man ! "

And the President said,

" Saving the Duke."

"The decrees which I made," said Deodonato, " I unmake. Henceforth let men
and maidens in my Duchy marry or not
marry as they will, and God give them joy
of it."

And all, save Fusbius, cried " Amen." But
Fusbius cried,

" Your Highness, it is demonstrated beyond cavil, ay, to the satisfaction of Your Highness——— "

" This is very tedious," said Deodonato. " Let him speak no more."

And again he drew near to Dulcissima, and there, before them all, he fell on his knee. And a murmur ran through the Hall.

" Madam," said Deodonato, " if you love me, wed me. And, if you love me not, depart in peace and in honour; and I, Deodonato, will live my life alone."

Then the damsel trembled, and barely did Deodonato catch her words :

" There are many men here," said she.

"It is not given to Princes," said Deodonato, " to be alone. Nevertheless, if you will, leave me alone."

Then the damsel bent low, so that the breath of her mouth stirred the hair on Deodonato's head, and he shivered as he knelt.

" My Prince and my King ! " said she.

And Deodonato shot to his feet, and before them all he kissed her, and, turning, spoke :

" As I have wooed, let every man in this Duchy woo. As I have won, let every man that is worthy win. For, unless he so woo, and unless he so win, vain is his wooing and vain is his winning, and a fig for his wedding, say I, Deodonato! I, that was Deodonato, and now am—Deodonato and Dulcissima."

And a great cheer rang out in the Hall, and Fusbius fled to the door; and they tore his gown as he went and cursed him for a knave. But the President raised his voice aloud and cried,

"May Heaven preserve Your Highnesses— and here's a blessing on all windows!"

And that is the reason why you will find (if you travel there, as I trust you may, for nowhere are the ladies fairer or the men so gallant) more windows in the Duchy of Deodonato than anywhere in the wide world besides. For the more windows, the wider the view; and the wider the view, the more pretty damsels do you see; and the more pretty damsels you see, the more jocund a thing is life; and that is what the men of the Duchy love—and not least Duke Deodonato, whom, with his bride Dulcissima, may Heaven long preserve!

THE END.

PRINTED BY WILLIAM CLOWES AND SONS, LIMITED, LONDON AND BECCLES.

SOME NEW NOVELS

PUBLISHED BY

A. D. INNES & CO.

By MAX PEMBERTON—
A GENTLEMAN'S GENTLEMAN.
Crown 8vo, cloth.   Illustrated by Sydney Cowell.   Price 6s.

By EDEN PHILPOTTS—
MY LAUGHING PHILOSOPHER.
Crown 8vo, cloth, illustrated.   Price 6s.

By G. B. BURGIN—
THE JUDGE OF THE FOUR CORNERS.
Crown 8vo, cloth.   Price 6s.

By FRANCIS GRIBBLE—
THE THINGS THAT MATTER.
Crown 8vo, cloth.   Price 6s.

By NORMA LORIMER—
A SWEET DISORDER.
Crown 8vo, cloth.   Price 6s.

By F. M. WHITE—
THE ROBE OF LUCIFER.
Crown 8vo, cloth.   Price 6s.

By HARRY LANDER—
STAGES IN THE JOURNEY.
Crown 8vo, cloth.   Price 3/6.

A. D. INNES & CO.'S NEW NOVELS.

By A NEW AUTHOR.

MISTRESS DOROTHY MARVIN. A Tale of the Seventeenth Century. By J. C. SNAITH. Being Excerpts from the Memoirs of Sir Edward Armstrong, Baronet, of Copeland Hall, in the County of Somerset. With Illustrations by S. COWELL. Second Edition. Crown 8vo, buckram, 6s.

The Speaker says :—"The author has succeeded in making his story intensely interesting. . . . One of the very best adventure stories we have had for a long time past."

By FRANK BARRETT, Author of " The Admirable Lady Biddy Fane."

A SET OF ROGUES : Namely, Christopher Sutton, John Dawson, the Señor Don Sanches del Castillo de Castelana, and Moll Dawson. Their Wicked Conspiracy, and a True Account of their Travels and Adventures. With Illustrations by S. COWELL. Crown 8vo, buckram, 6s.

The Pall Mall Gazette says :—"He has related the adventures of a set of rogues with so pliant a tongue and in such attractive fashion that it is impossible for mere flesh and blood to resist them. . . . His set of rogues have won our entire sympathy, and his narrative our hearty approval."

By JAMES CHALMERS.

THE RENEGADE : Being a Novel dealing with the Career of the American Captain Paul Jones. With Illustrations by JOHN WILLIAMSON. Crown 8vo, buckram, price 6s.

The Scotsman says :—" . . . The author shows real power as a writer of romance, and there are passages which would not have been unworthy of Scott himself. The book . . . displays remarkable power, and the author ought to make his mark as a writer of stories of adventure and romance."

By the late MRS. J. K. SPENDER, Author of " Thirteen Doctors," &c.

THE WOOING OF DORIS. Crown 8vo, cloth, 6s.

The World says :—" Has much to recommend it to novel-readers. A clever plot, well-drawn characters . . . such are the leading features of a novel by which the reputation of its much regretted writer is fully sustained to the last."

By LESLIE KEITH, Author of " The Chilcotes," " Lisbeth," &c.

FOR LOVE OF PRUE. Crown 8vo, cloth, 6s.

The Glasgow Herald says :—" An uncommonly clever novel . . . deserves to find numerous and appreciative readers."

By ARTHUR RICKETT.

LOST CHORDS : Being Some Emotions without Morals. Crown 8vo, cloth, 2s. 6d. net.

Punch says :—" A practical joke capitally carried out by author and publisher."

LONDON : A. D. INNES & CO., 31 & 32, Bedford Street, Strand.